"Get her before she reaches you!"
roared Chad.

Gil hesitated. The squaw closed in. Gil
jumped to one side but did not fire.
Chad fired up the slope and hit her in
the back. She fell without moving. Gil
ran to her and bent down. Her knife fanged
upward and caught him across the face.

Blood spurted brightly as the kid staggered
back, dropping his rifle. Chad charged
up the slope and fired point-blank into
the squaw's back.

Gil stood there with a dirty hand clamped
to the side of his face, blood leaking
between his fingers. "She was a
woman," he said huskily.

Chad spat to one side. "Some of them
are worse than the bucks," he said.

Fawcett Gold Medal Books
by Gordon D. Shirreffs:

SHOWDOWN
IN SONORA

Gordon D. Shirreffs

FAWCETT GOLD MEDAL • NEW YORK

SHOWDOWN IN SONORA

Published by Fawcett Gold Medal Books, a unit of CBS Publications, the Consumer Publishing Division of CBS Inc.

ISBN: 0-449-12710-9

Printed in the United States of America

12   11   10   9   8   7   6   5   4   3

ONE

LEE KERSHAW PUT a strain on the rusted strand of barbed wire. It tightened beautifully and Lee gave a grunt of satisfaction as he stepped back from the fence. The taut wire snapped, coiling back like an aroused rattlesnake to strike at Lee's face. He caught the vicious lash of the wire with his forearm and gloved hand to protect his lean face. "Sonofabitch," he said with deep feeling.

Anselmo Campos limped back from the fence while feeling within his waistband for his tobacco canteen. "It is as I have so often said, *patrón,*" he said in his soft Spanish. "This wire is not even fit for junk. We have wasted the whole day on it."

"The years rob you of your skill, old one," countered Lee. He instantly regretted it. The old man was right. That was the trouble—he was almost *always* right.

Anselmo's one good eye was fixed on Lee. "It was not this way in your father's time and in the time of your grandfather." He shaped a cigarette with his work-gnarled fingers.

Lee looked along the line of the old fence. Warped fence poles sagged with the weight of the rusted wire. Some poles had broken off short and hung suspended by the wire. They swayed in the dry wind that swept across the rolling New Mexico hills.

"In your father's time, and that of *his* father," continued the old vaquero relentlessly, "there was not a broken wire that was not fixed as soon as it was seen. I remember——"

Lee spat dryly. "You remember too goddamned much, old man, and do too little work."

Anselmo tossed the rawhide tobacco canteen to Lee. "A

5

man who worked for your father and your grandfather was treated with dignity, *patrón*," he said.

Jesus Christ, thought Lee, here we go again! He shaped a quirly and lighted it. When he had returned to the old Barbed K after an absence of years, he had never expected to find any of the old Kershaw *corrida* still there, but Anselmo had been there, as he had been for two generations.

"For almost fifty years," reminisced the old man, "this has been Kershaw land."

"Less five years," reminded Lee.

The one good eye sort of wandered toward Lee. "For no good reason, *patrón*." A bright tear slid out of the milkwhite sightless eye. "God knows it," Anselmo piously added.

Lee whistled sharply to his chestnut. Anselmo stiffly mounted his old gray. The two of them rode away from that triple-accursed fence. The horses footed easily down the long slope while the dry wind swept across it, rippling the yellowed grasses so that they looked like waves pushing busily toward the distant shoreline of the hills. There was an endless drifting of puffed white clouds across the bright blue sky, following each other like docile sheep toward the rose and gold mural of the setting sun. Lee began to forget his rasped irritation as he looked at the sunset and the vast and lonely beauty of the land.

"*Querencia*," murmured Anselmo. He did not look at Lee. "It is said that one who is born here must return here to live out the remainder of his life or he will never be satisfied no matter where he wanders."

"Brandy talk," grunted Lee. *Querencia*—an affection, a longing; a favorite spot or haunt. Oh, he knew well enough what the old vaquero meant all right. It had been Lee's grandmother who had named the valley in west central New Mexico long before the Civil War. When Lee's grandfather had settled there the area had still been part of Mexico. She had named the area well—so well, in fact, that the name *Barbed K* and *Querencia* had been interchangeable for many years until at last *Querencia*

6

only was used to designate both the valley and the ranch.

"Fifty years this has been Kershaw land," murmured Anselmo.

"Less five," corrected Lee.

"It need not have been that way, *patrón*," said Anselmo.

Lee shot a hard glance at the old man. "The Prodigal Son, eh, old one?" he asked to soften his temper.

Anselmo shrugged. "A son's place is with his father, on his father's land. So it is said in the Bible."

Lee grinned crookedly. "If a man has a hundred sheep and one of them strays away, will not the shepherd leave the ninety and nine upon the hills and go in search of the one that is astray? And if he happens to find it, I tell you he rejoices more over it than over the ninety and nine that did not go astray."

"Do not mock me, *patrón*," replied Anselmo quietly.

"The Gospel according to Matthew," said Lee relentlessly.

"The *patrón* knows I cannot read," said the old vaquero.

"But your memory is long, eh, old one? I know what you are thinking! I left the Querencia at a time when my father's health was failing and he wasn't able to keep up the place as he had done before and as it was done in my grandfather's time! Was that my fault?"

"I will not answer that," replied the old man.

They skirted one of the waterholes. The water was low, leaving a wide margin of trampled mud about it. It had been an exceptionally dry season. The creek to the west was running low, dotting its sinuous course with shallow pools that were green with scum.

"The windmill must soon be fixed, *patrón*," Anselmo suggested.

"You told me that yesterday and the day before that."

"It has not been fixed, *patrón*."

"There hasn't been time!" snapped Lee.

"There will be a new moon tonight. It will be like daylight."

7

There was no reply to Anselmo's argument. Lee check-reined his temper. If only the old one could be wrong—just once, that was all Lee wanted.

The sun was dying behind the western mountains as the two men rode down the last long slope toward the ranch buildings. There was something missing—in sight and sound. The familiar whirring of the old Halladay Standard windmill did not come to the two men on the dry wind, nor could they see the gaunt, rusted structure. They rounded a sagging barn. "Gawdammittohell!" roared Lee. The windmill had collapsed into tangled, rusted ruin atop the stock tank, smashing the tank sides into the ground. The released water stained the dry ground.

Anselmo was wise enough to keep his *boca* shut as he took the two horses. He was on his way to his quarters behind the rambling ranch house when Lee called out to him. "Come and stay in the house tonight, old man."

Anselmo shook his white head. "It is not my place, *patrón*."

"Well, one can at least eat with me, old one."

Anselmo hesitated. "I am not hungry, *patrón*. When one is as old as I am, there is little hunger for fighting, eating, and women."

Lee grinned. "There is brandy, hombre! Eh?"

Anselmo did not lose his native dignity. "A *copita* will suffice, *patrón*. Only one, mind you."

Lee walked in through the front door and lighted a cracked-cylindered Rayo table lamp. The gathering soft light revealed that one of the ceiling vigas had cracked and sagged that day. Lee went outside and got a peeled pole from the pile he had accumulated to repair the corral fence. It was something else he hadn't quite gotten around to doing. He propped up the viga. A shower of hard earth pattered down. Lee cursed softly as he jumped aside to avoid a squirming straw-colored scorpion that nearly struck his face. A bootheel ground the creature into a malodorous pulp. The roof would have to be rebuilt before the fall rains.

His bootheels popped and echoed in the hallway as he

walked back to the kitchen. A field mouse scurried into cover as he lighted the Argand table lamp. "Anselmo!" he called out.

The rusted screen door creaked open and the old man came in with his hat in his hand. Lee filled a water glass with Jerez brandy and jerked a thumb toward a chair. Anselmo sat down and took the glass. "*Gracias,*" he murmured.

"*Por nada.*" Lee picked up the bottle between two strong fingers and held it to his mouth. He lowered the bottle and looked at Anselmo. "I'm beginning to understand the look my father used to have on his face in the days when I was more concerned with booze, women, and gambling than I was about his health and the finances of the Querencia."

Anselmo waved a hand. "You were young and a fool," he said. "They are one and the same." He sipped a little brandy and belched politely. "Still, your good father, may God rest his soul, never said much about your wild ways until the shooting trouble in Cibola, *patrón.*"

Lee got a huge slab of steak and cut it into two pieces. He wet it, floured, salted, and peppered it, and placed it to one side while he lighted the stove and placed the Dutch oven atop it, dropping pieces of trimmed steak fat into the oven. He sat silently with the old man while the stove heated, cracking now and then as the metal expanded. Lee glanced covertly at Anselmo. The old one was the last of the Querencia corrida and Lee was the last of the Kershaws, and it seemed as though the two of them sat there haunting the old estancia. It was almost as though they did not exist.

When the fat began to sizzle, Lee plopped the floured and seasoned steak into the Dutch oven. He seared both sides of the steak and then placed the heavy lid atop the oven. He mixed tomatoes and corn together and placed the saucepan on the stove.

Anselmo opened his one good eye. "One is used to eating and thinking alone," he murmured. "Thirteen years, eh, *patrón?*"

Lee nodded. Thirteen long years of trails dotted with blackened fire sites in the lonely places from New Mexico to Texas, and from Chihuahua to Sonora and Arizona.

"But now one is home, eh, *patrón*?" asked Anselmo.

"Querencia," murmured Lee. He drank on that.

Anselmo suddenly raised his head. "Someone comes," he said. "He rides hard. The devil is at his heels, that one."

Lee looked quickly at the old man. Lee had ears like an Apache, but he had heard nothing. Lee walked to the rear door and walked out under the sagging ramada and then to the end of the warped porch to look toward the road. There was a faint promise of the new moon in the eastern sky. The steady drumming of hoofs on the hard-packed road came from the northwest. There was low rolling thunder as the hoofs struck the worn planking of the bridge. The horseman slowed down as he neared the gate to the estancia. He swung down from the saddle.

Lee catfooted toward the front of the house and stood under the deep shadows of the ramada. The horseman opened the gate and led the hard-blowing horse through it. Lee caught the quick movement of the man's head as he looked toward the corral where Anselmo's gray and Lee's chestnut, light bay, and coyote dun mounts were kept. He started toward the corral.

"Stand where you are!" Lee warned and just as he did so he remembered he had left his gun belt and holstered six-shooter in the kitchen.

The man whirled and moved like a cat to get his horse between himself and Lee. "That you, Lee?" he called out.

"Hello, Chad," replied Lee.

"You alone, amigo?" asked Chad.

"Anselmo Campos is in the kitchen getting drunk on my brandy," answered Lee.

Chad laughed. "That's the same as being alone."

"You sound nervous," said Lee.

Chad walked easily toward the house accompanied by the soft silvery chiming of his spurs. "Just a little tired, Lee."

"You came from Cibola? That's not a long ride."

Chad shook his head. "You're pretty isolated out here," he observed.

"Are you asking me or telling me?" Lee grinned. "You're the first visitor we've had in weeks." He held out his hand and gripped that of Chad. "I'll turn your horse in with mine. You'll stay for supper?"

Chad did not answer. He looked back over his shoulder toward the road. He tethered his sorrel to a ramada post. The pleasing odor of the cooking food drifted to both men. Lee walked in through the front door followed by Chad. Chad looked about the big room and at the prop that held up the viga. He grinned. "You have enough of this estancia yet?" he asked.

Lee did not answer as he walked on through to the kitchen and took the corned tomatoes from the stove. He filled a coffeepot with water. "Grub is about ready," he said over his shoulder. "Time for a drink first."

Chad picked up the bottle and upended it. He lowered the bottle and slewed his gray eyes sideways at Lee. "Mother's milk," he murmured. "You didn't answer my question."

"Set and eat," Lee said.

"I'm heading south," said Chad. "Chihuahua way. I need a compañero to side me, Lee."

"I hope you find one," replied Lee. He looked sideways at Chad. "Why Chihuahua?"

Chad flashed his charming, infectious grin. "Lopez is starting another revolution," he answered.

"Which one is this?" asked Lee. "Number Six or Number Seven?"

"You ought to know, if anyone does," Chad answered. "They'll get him this time. He ran out his luck a couple of revolutions back."

"He'll pay fifty dollars a day—in gold," Chad urged. "He's bound to win this time, Lee. For a time at least."

Lee shook his head. "I'm staying here, amigo."

Chad grinned. "I didn't believe it months past when all the talk around Cibola was about Lee Kershaw buying

11

back the old Querencia from Bennett Luscombe, of all people, and setting hisself up as a rancher with one old, broken-down vaquero and fifty head of stock. It is to laugh!"

"I was born here," said Lee quietly.

"Querencia! Is that it? You must be getting old."

Lee slanted his hard blue eyes at the younger man. "That's fool's talk," he warned.

"You're fighting a hopeless battle here, Lee. Everyone knows Luscombe took your money and he'll foreclose on you the first chance he gets."

"I've kept up with the payments," said Lee.

Chad picked up the bottle. He grinned. "*Have* you?" he murmured.

Lee took off the top of the dutch oven. "Steak's about ready," he said. He heard the faint chiming of spurs. He looked over the head of the dozing Anselmo toward the hallway. Lee filled two plates with steak and corned tomatoes. Chad Mercer was on the run again. Lee could almost see a reflection of himself in Chad Mercer. Chad had been a skinny, grinning kid when he had attached himself to Lee like a sand burr to a saddle blanket. He couldn't be insulted, driven away, or *kicked* away, until he had learned all Lee could teach him. He had learned fast and well—*too damned* well, thought Lee.

Chad came back through the hallway. "I'll need a fresh horse," he said. "I'll need food and brandy too."

"Stay the night. Your sorrel will be all right in the morning," replied Lee. He sat down at the table and refilled Anselmo's glass. Anselmo opened his one good eye, took the glass in a steady hand and drank deeply. He placed the glass on the table, wiped his mouth, closed his eye, and dozed off again. Lee did not look up at Chad.

"Maybe you didn't understand me," suggested Chad.

Lee looked up. "Set and eat," he invited. His eyes held those of the younger man.

Chad sat down opposite Lee, never taking his eyes from him. He sawed quickly at his steak and stuffed his mouth, chewing vigorously. "You know I'm on the run," he mumbled around the steak.

Lee nodded.

"Aren't you going to ask why?"

Lee shook his head.

Chad swallowed. "Then I get the horse?"

Lee eyed the younger man. "No," he quietly replied.

It was very quiet in the big kitchen. Wood snapped in the big range. Anselmo belched softly. Chad lowered his hands to his lap. "Why, Lee?" he asked.

"I can't afford to take that risk," replied Lee. "They'll know you came here, expecting me to help you. I can't afford it, kid."

Chad's face was hard and cold-looking. "You can say I stole the horse."

Lee shook his head. "They won't buy that."

"It's because you owe Luscombe money, isn't it?"

Lee shook his head again. "Look, Chad," he said in a low voice. "I've come back here after all these years to rebuild the Querencia. I've had enough of your kind of life, always on the move, sometimes on the run, and I want no more of it. ¿Comprende?"

Chad nodded. "And Bennett Luscombe is also sheriff, is that it? Doesn't that throw a little weight, Lee? Come on! Admit it to your old compañero."

Lee began to saw at a piece of steak. "Old is right," he agreed. "Past tense, amigo. Like I said: I can't afford to take the risk."

"In short," said Chad. "You can't afford my friendship."

Lee looked up. "You've got the idea, kid."

Something clicked crisply under the table. Chad smiled, but there was no mirth in his clear gray eyes. "Just get up nice and easy like, hombre," he ordered. "Keep your hands high!"

"I'm unarmed," said Lee as he stood up.

Chad laughed. "You? There never has been a time in the past fifteen years that you've been unarmed."

"You forget the times we were in jail together," Lee said dryly.

"Fill a sack with food, hombre," Chad ordered.

Lee obediently did as he was told. "Put in some brandy," said Chad. He grinned. "I see a shelffull of it in that

13

cabinet." He lighted a cigarette. "Now take the sack out to the back porch."

Lee walked through the bright moonlight to the barn with Chad behind him leading the sorrel. "Put my saddle on that good-looking light bay," ordered Chad. Lee unsaddled the tired sorrel. The horse blanket was stinking stiff and ridged with sweat-caked dust. He passed a hand along the sorrel's bare back and shook his head. Lee roped and saddled the bay. "Lead it to the back of the casa," ordered Chad. Lee led the bay to the house.

"You've still got time to join me," suggested Chad. "Lopez can sure use the both of us."

Lee stowed the food and brandy in the saddlebags. He slowly shook his head. "Lopez still owes me over five hundred 'dobe dollars," said Lee.

"Why not come along and collect it?"

"No," said Lee. He eyed the younger man.

"*Querencia,* eh?" Chad shrugged in disgust.

Lee moved like a cat, striking out with his left hand to drive Chad's gun hand sideways while he swung a looping right to the jaw. The horse was startled. He threw his head sideways, striking Lee alongside the head, staggering Lee. Chad leaped to one side and as Lee fell sideways Chad swung the gun. The barrel clipped Lee across the side of the head and he went down on his hands and knees, half stunned.

"You sonofabitch!" snapped Chad.

"They'll get you," Lee grunted.

"Ain't no man alive can catch me before I reach the border!" rapped out Chad. "Not even you, Kershaw!"

Lee shook his head. "You're safe on that bet," he said. "My manhunting days are over and you'd better, by God, be glad about that!"

The bootheel thudded alongside Lee's jaw, driving him sideways to the ground. He raised his head and the gun barrel came down with crushing force atop his head. Dimly he heard the thudding of hoofs and the sound of laughter and then his face struck the ground and he went off the deep end into nothingness.

TWO

THE MOON WAS slanting down toward the west when Lee raised his head. He instantly regretted it. A stabbing pain shot through his skull. He sat up, swaying with the effort, and gingerly touched the side and top of his head, feeling the blood that matted his reddish hair. He touched the side of his jaw and then gently worked the lower jaw back and forth. It should have been broken. He got to his feet and pain lanced through his head. He walked slowly to the washstand behind the kitchen and wiped the blood from his hair and face. There was a welt alongside his skull and an egg atop it and his jaw was swelling. He turned and looked toward the hills to the southeast. He touched his head and spat to one side. "You could have had the horse without breaking my skull," he said quietly.

Lee walked into the kitchen. The old man dozed in his chair. Lee shoved him to one side and caught him before he fell to the floor. He raised Anselmo up to his shoulders and carried him to the one-roomed jacal where the old vaquero insisted on staying by himself. Lee kicked open a rolled-up pair of *colchones* and placed Anselmo atop them. "Sleep well, old man," he said as he closed the door.

Lee walked back into the house and drank deeply, wiping his mouth with the back of a hand. Suddenly he raised his head. The faint drumming of hooves came from the road, but this time there were many horses. "Figures," murmured Lee. He drank again and placed his hat atop his head, slanting it over the welt. He walked through the echoing hallway and opened the front door in time to see six horsemen ride through the gateway. One of them slid from his saddle and pulled a rifle free from its scabbard, working the lever to load the weapon as he catfooted toward the corral. He peered over the top rail and then turned to nod toward the other horsemen.

Lee stood in the shadow of the ramada and shaped a cigarette. The rest of the horsemen dismounted and took their rifles, fanning out into a sort of skirmish line. One man walked forward and waved on the others. Lee lighted up and stepped off the porch into the clear moonlight. "He's gone!" he called out. One of the men threw up his rifle and aimed it. "Stop that, you damned idiot!" called out Bennett Luscombe. Luscombe walked toward the house, turning once to look back at his men, and as he did so the moonlight shone dully on his sheriff's star.

"He's getting a good lead," suggested Lee. "Don't waste your time here, Sheriff."

Luscombe nodded. "And he got a fresh mount from you, his old compañero," he said coldly.

"He *took* it, if that's what you mean," said Lee.

One of the men laughed.

Luscombe felt inside his coat for his cigar case. He selected a cigar and clipped off the end with a silver cutter attached to his watch chain. He placed the cigar in his mouth and lighted a match, passing it slowly back and forth across the blunt tip of the cigar and all the time his fine dark eyes never left the face of Lee Kershaw.

"He rode in here an hour and a half ago," said Lee. "Wanted a fresh horse. I refused him. He forced me at gunpoint to switch his saddle to my light bay, then slugged me and bootheeled my jaw to lay me out."

"Hear, hear," said one of the men.

Lee looked past Luscombe. "You've got a big mouth," he said.

Luscombe rubbed his smoothly shaven jaw. "You must admit that it does sound a little farfetched," he suggested.

Lee took off his hat. "See for yourself," he invited.

Luscombe shook his head. "Somehow I can't imagine anyone, even Chad Mercer, getting the bulge on you, Kershaw."

"I always said Mercer was the better man," said a broad-shouldered man.

"Shit!" snapped a short posseman. "Mercer ain't half the gunslick Kershaw is!"

"He got the bulge on him, like Mr. Luscombe said, didn't he?" countered another man.

Luscombe turned slowly. "For Christ's sake," he said slowly. "What have I got for a posse? A bunch of bums from the Cibola saloons?"

"You might be just right at that," Lee suggested.

"Why, damn you!" barked the broad-shouldered man.

"Keep out of this, Beatty!" ordered Luscombe. "Send Manuel toward those hills behind the ranch buildings. There should be some tracks there."

"The ground is as dry as last night's whiskey bottle," said Lee.

Luscombe turned. "Manuel will find a trace," he said confidently.

Lee watched Manuel out of the corners of his eyes. He knew him—part Indian, part Mex, and maybe part Negro. Some said his father had been a Negro trooper from Fort Defiance. Some claimed he could track a ghost through a snowstorm. "He'll have his hands full tracking Mercer," said Lee.

Luscombe nodded. "Which way was he heading?"

Lee shrugged. "Mexico, he said. Chihuahua, most likely."

"You wouldn't lie about that?"

"No," replied Lee quietly.

Luscombe turned. "Beatty," he said. The broad-shouldered man came forward. "Take your men after Manuel. Leave Gil here with me. Stick to Mercer's trail. He'll likely be heading toward the San Mateos. I'll wire ahead from Cibola to Silver City and have the message relayed to Las Cruces and El Paso. Keep pushing him, Beatty. Tire him out. Kill your horses if you have to, *but tire him out!* Understand?"

Beatty nodded. He led his men around the side of the building, leaving a tall young man standing there watching Lee.

Luscombe glanced at the young man. "My son Gil, Kershaw," he said. "You remember him?"

Lee nodded. "He was about six years old the last time I saw him. A snotty-nosed kid always in the tow of his redheaded sister, Leila."

"Watch yourself, Kershaw," warned Gil.

Lee grinned. "The boy has grown into a man," he said.

"You'd better know it!" snapped Gil.

Lee shrugged. "He isn't much like Frank, Mr. Luscombe, is he?"

Luscombe's face tightened. "Frank is dead," he said.

Lee narrowed his eyes. "Frank dead? I can't believe that."

"You'd better," said Gil. "It was Chad Mercer that murdered him."

"For the love of God!" said Lee.

Luscombe nodded. "It happened months back."

"And you're just after Mercer now?" asked Lee.

"We just got conclusive evidence," answered Luscombe. He studied Lee. "And you let him have a horse to escape on. Aiding and abetting, Kershaw. Accessory after the fact."

"You're still more of the lawyer than the sheriff," said Lee quietly. "You know I didn't let him have that horse willingly. Look at my head, dammit! Does that look like I wanted to help him?"

"Doesn't mean a damned thing," said Gil.

"Shut up, Gil!" snapped his father. He looked toward the house. "Have you got any coffee, Kershaw?" he asked.

"Be my guest," said Lee. He led the way into the house.

Luscombe glanced at the prop that held up the ceiling viga. "Good God," he murmured.

"Home, Sweet Home," added Gil.

Lee stocked up the fire and placed the coffeepot on the stove top. "There's brandy there," he suggested.

Luscombe shook his head as Gil eagerly reached for the bottle. "Not on duty, son," he said. "You've been sworn in as deputy."

"Just one, Dad?" asked Gil.

"You heard me!" said his father. He looked at Lee. "You working the Querencia alone?" he asked.

"I've got Anselmo Campos," replied Lee as he took a drink.

"That's like nothing," said Luscombe.

"I'm very capable," countered Lee. He sat down opposite Luscombe. "Now, what's on your mind, Sheriff?"

Luscombe smiled faintly. "Direct and to the point. The Kershaw way, is that it?"

Lee nodded. "You knew my father well," he said. He raised his eyes and studied Luscombe.

Luscombe nodded. "I owed him a great deal. He paved the way for me in this country when I came to Cibola with a fresh, unused degree in law and a patch on the seat of my trousers."

"And you foreclosed on him when you had the chance," added Lee.

"Business is business," threw in Gil.

"Is he always like that?" asked Lee.

Luscombe shrugged. "He'll learn. It was Frank who had the brains. He would have done well."

"Not your way," said Lee. "Frank was a straight shooter."

Luscombe's face tightened a little. "You're in one hell of a spot, Kershaw," he declared. "You're in hock two payments on the Querencia. You're not making a go of it. You're under suspicion of aiding and abetting an escaped murderer."

"Go on," suggested Lee. "You're leading up to a point which certainly won't benefit me."

"It might," said Luscombe. He relighted his cigar and idly fanned out the match. "You've always been a loser, Kershaw. A drifter. A hired gunfighter. You've never really stuck to anything. Deputy Sheriff in Cochise County, Arizona Territory, Texas Ranger, stock detective, bounty hunter, mercenary fighting for Lopez down in Mexico." Luscombe leaned back in his chair. "Strange, too, that whenever you rode alone, you rode on the side of the law, and when you rode with Chad Mercer, it was usually on the wrong side of the law."

19

"Such as?" asked Lee.

"Fighting for Lopez," answered Luscombe.

"That's not illegal in this country," said Lee.

"It is in Mexico. It's not really important. I said you were a loser and had really never stuck to anything. That's not quite right. There's *one* thing you do well, better than most men, perhaps better than *any* man in the Southwest. That's manhunting! You're no rancher, Kershaw! *Manhunter!* That's your game!"

Lee stood up and took the coffeepot from the stove. "Get to the point," he said over his shoulder. "You want me to track down Chad Mercer for you, is that it?"

"Yes," admitted Luscombe.

"Morgan Beatty is capable and he's got that damned human bloodhound Manuel with him."

"He won't catch Mercer and you know it."

Lee filled three coffee cups and placed them on the table. "I taught Mercer all he knows," he said, almost as though to himself.

"All the more reason you should take on the job."

Lee shook his head.

"Worried about your reputation, Kershaw?" challenged Gil.

"It was your father who mentioned reputation," replied Lee. "Not me." He studied the kid. "It's a reputation not easily earned and it isn't one a man can shake off very easily."

Gil smiled irritatingly. "Maybe that's why Lee Kershaw, the great manhunter, is hiding out on the Querencia, on a broken-down old estancia, with a broken-down old vaquero for help," he suggested.

"Shut up, Gil," ordered Bennett Luscombe. He leaned forward. "Now, listen here, Kershaw, and you listen well! I have every legal right to foreclose on you right now."

"You play a hard game," said Lee.

"It's not a game. It's *business,*" retorted Luscombe. "Now, I want Mercer and I mean to have him. I can run you in right now for aiding and abetting him to escape, and you'd lose the Querencia to boot. Will you agree to track down Mercer and bring him back to Cibola?"

"What's in this for me, as long as we're talking business?" asked Lee.

"I won't foreclose. I'll give you an extension, all notarized and legal, on that."

"It might take a long time," said Lee quietly.

"All expenses paid, courtesy of the county."

Lee looked down at his coffee cup. "Professionals come high, Mr. Luscombe. You should know that from the size of your lawyer's fees."

Gil grinned. "You've hit a tender spot, Kershaw," he said.

Luscombe shot a hard glance at his son. "How much do you want, Kershaw?" he asked.

Lee laced his coffee with brandy. "A thousand in my hand for a starter. You know that's my usual fee. That's for *one* week. Thereafter, for every additional week, I want five hundred dollars."

"You're a damned pirate!" barked the sheriff.

Lee shrugged. "You want Mercer, don't you?"

"The county won't stand for that."

Lee looked up at him. "*They* won't, but *you* will."

"How do you want to handle this? Bounty hunter? Deputy-Sheriff?"

"You want to *legalize* it, then?" asked Lee.

"The decision is yours. It would be better that way."

Lee nodded. "I'll take a deputy's star," he said.

Luscombe reached inside his coat and withdrew a heavy, legal-size manila envelope and a small leather case. "Stand up," he said. "Hold up your right hand." He looked at Gil. "You're witness," he added. He swore in Lee, opened the leather box, and removed a deputy-sheriff's star from it and pinned it on Lee's shirt. He handed Lee the envelope. "There's the warrant and the thousand, Kershaw."

"You certainly plan ahead," observed Lee dryly.

"That's my way of business," said Luscombe. He smiled faintly. "You see, Kershaw, I'm a professional too."

Lee drained his coffee cup. "I'll leave tonight," he said.

Luscombe nodded. "He'll be moving fast."

Lee smiled ruefully. "He's riding a damned good horse."

Luscombe turned to Gil. "Get started back to Cibola." He took out paper and pen and quickly wrote a message, which he then handed to Gil. "Get moving! I want this message in Silver City, Las Cruces, and El Paso before Mercer is beyond the San Mateos." The kid walked to the hall door and then turned to look at Lee. "You sure you're not too old to be taking on a young man like Chad Mercer?" he asked.

"Get to hell out of here!" snapped his father.

The kid grinned as he beat a retreat down the hallway.

Lee walked outside and roped the chestnut and then his good dun. He saddled the chestnut and led both horses to the rear of the ranch house. While Luscombe sat at the table drinking coffee and smoking a fresh cigar Lee changed into his trail clothing. He placed pommel and cantle rolls on the chestnut and filled the saddlebags, finally sheathing his Winchester '76 in the saddle scabbard. He turned to see Luscombe watching him from the kitchen porch. "I'll send out a couple of hands to keep the place," the sheriff said.

Lee shook his head. "Anselmo is here. What there is to be done, he can do. If anything happens to me, see that the old man gets the money due me."

Luscomb nodded. "If you meet up with Beatty, tell him I said you should take Manuel with you."

Lee swung up into the saddle. "Manuel, *shit!*" he said. "I work alone."

Luscombe looked toward the north. "Wind is shifting," he observed. "Winter's coming on."

Lee shrugged. "I'm heading south. Like the birds." He kneed the chestnut away from the house. "By the way," he added. "How do you want him?"

Luscombe was puzzled. "What do you mean?"

"Dead or alive? That's the usual phrase, isn't it?"

"It's in the warrant," replied the sheriff.

Lee rested an elbow on the pommel pack. "I meant you personally," he said.

"Alive of course," replied Luscombe.

"But either way if necessary?"

Luscombe relighted his cigar and eyed Lee over the flare of the match. His eyes were enigmatical. "That's really up to you, isn't it, *manhunter?*"

Lee touched the chestnut with his heels and rode toward the slopes beyond the estancia. At the top of the ridge he drew rein and looked back and down at the ranch buildings. The lights were still on and he saw Luscombe's shadow pass between a window and the kitchen lamp. Suddenly Lee raised his head. The wind brought the distant sound of horse's hoofs to him. There was more than one horse, two or more, perhaps, and they were moving fast in the darkness south along the valley road. No one lived up that way. It was Querencia range almost to the western edge of the San Mateos. Lee felt for the makings and shaped a cigarette. He lighted it and touched the chestnut with his heels. He looked toward the southwest, along the dark trough of the Querencia Valley, but the sound of the hoofbeats had died away.

Somewhere on the western rim of the valley a coyote howled his heart out at the last light of the moon. Lee rode toward the southeast. Somehow that coyote didn't quite sound like a coyote. An omen maybe, the thought drifted eerily through Lee's mind as he rode southeast on the trail of the man who had once been his greatest friend.

THREE

THE WIND WAS shifting with the coming of the dawn, dying away and then reviving itself only to die away again. It was dark in the valley and the trees swayed and murmured in the fitful wind. The sound of the hoofbeats echoed hollowly from the valley sides. The pungent odor of woodsmoke came to Lee Kershaw. He reined in the chestnut. To his right up a wide draw there appeared a red eye winking out of the darkness. Lee slid from the saddle and unsheathed his Winchester. The chestnut whinnied.

"Who's out there?" called out a man. Boots grated on the hard ground.

"Lee Kershaw, Beatty," replied Lee.

"Come on, then! We're damned glad you came!"

Lee led the two horses toward the winking red eye. Wood was thrown on the fire. A flicker of flame ran along the branches and then they burst into flame. Three men were revealed in the uncertain light and then another appeared carrying an armload of squaw wood. The tracker Manuel stood to one side. He was hatless and a dirty bandage was wrapped around his thick shock of hair. There were no horses in sight, nor did they sound off at the chestnut and dun.

Lee halted. "What happened to the human bloodhound?" he asked.

"Mercer backtrailed on us, Kershaw," explained Beatty. "Me, Jed, and Ben was getting some sleep while Manuel stood guard. Mercer cold-cocked Manuel and run off our horses."

"Didn't he leave my bay?" asked Lee.

"He left us nothing but a couple piles of horseshit!" snapped the deputy.

Lee eyed the sullen tracker. "Slap some of it on his cabeza," he suggested. "The heat and moisture will draw out the swelling. My ol' granny taught me that."

"He run off with our grub too," complained Jed.

Lee unhooked his coffee canteen from his saddle and tossed it to Jed. "Heat that up," he suggested.

Beatty narrowed his eyes. He studied the cantle and pommel packs and the full saddlebags. "You pulling out of the Querencia?" he asked.

Lee began to shape a cigarette. "Sort of," he admitted.

"You got a charge against you, you know," reminded Beatty.

Lee nodded. He tossed his tobacco canteen to Ben and then lighted his cigarette.

"What are you doing out here anyways?" asked Beatty.

"Tailing Mr. Mercer," replied Lee.

"Why?" shot out Beatty.

Lee turned the lapel of his coat to reveal his star. "I've got a warrant for Mercer," he explained.

"Bueno!" cried Beatty. "You can give us one of them horses. I'll send Jed back to Cibola for fresh mounts and some supplies."

"It's a long walk," said Lee easily.

Beatty took a step forward. "What the hell do you mean?" he demanded.

"By the time you get on after Mercer, his trail will be so cold you will be able to chill beer on it."

"He was here just a couple hours past!"

"Sure, sure," agreed Lee, "but meanwhile he's riding one of those horses to death and he'll switch on to another one and ride him to death. He rides like a Comanche! By the time he shifts his saddle to the third horse, he'll be damned near out of this county, and all the time you'll be sitting here on your ass moaning about the dirty trick he did to you."

Beatty flushed. His mouth worked a little under his thick dragoon mustache. "I'll still take one of those horses," he insisted.

Lee shook his head.

"Jed! Ben! Manuel!" snapped Beatty. The three of them closed in on Lee. Manuel suddenly jumped catlike to one side and raised his rifle. Jed plunged toward Lee while Ben circled around to get at the horses. Beatty freed his Colt from leather and circled around behind Jed and Manuel. Lee purposely dropped his rifle. He gripped the breed's rifle barrel and dragged it toward himself and at the same time he thrust out his long left leg. Manuel plunged headlong over the leg and hit the hard ground with a breath expelling grunt, releasing his hold on the rifle. Lee stomped back over the breed's body heedless of his raking spurs and then Lee swung the rifle sideways at

Jed. Jed went low to get under the rifle barrel, grinning at his wisdom and caught a bootheel in the privates that wiped the grin from his face. He doubled over in agony, dropping his hands to his crotch. Lee tapped him hard and sure across the nape of the neck with the rifle barrel and at the same time he brought up a knee against Jed's jaw. The posseman staggered sideways and sat down in the roaring fire. He rose phoenixlike from the flames, shrieking in agony and frustration and not knowing which to grab at first—his privates, his neck, his jaw, or his flame-seared rump. He rolled sideways on the ground squealing like a pig, beating at his rump with both hands.

Lee whirled, levering out the chambered round to make sure the rifle was loaded and reloading in one liquid movement. He held the heavy repeater at hip level. "Let go that dun," he ordered.

Ben looked into those cold blue eyes and backed away hastily from the dun. Beatty slowly raised his hands. His eyes flicked, giving him away. Lee whirled to meet Manuel's silent knife-tipped charge. There was no time for niceties. Lee reversed the rifle and drove the metal shod butt against Manuel's dark face. The butt plate toe ripped through skin and flesh and brought out a blood freshet. Lee kicked Manuel in the guts and as the breed went down Lee kicked out with his left foot and connected solidly against the side of Manuel's jaw with his bootheel. Something broke. The breed lay still.

Lee turned. He was hardly breathing rapidly. "Get your hands off that cutter," he ordered Beatty.

Beatty dropped the six-shooter and slowly raised his hands. His broad face worked. "I order you to turn over one of them horses to me," he said huskily. Fear showed in his flat eyes.

"You shit too, you bastard!" snapped Lee. "Get to hell away from those horses! Pronto! *Andale!*"

"You're interfering with an officer of the law in the performance of his duty!" shrieked the deputy.

Lee retrieved his tobacco canteen and coffee canteen. "I can say the same about you," he retorted.

"We're all in this together, ain't we?" demanded Beatty.

Lee rapidly worked the lever of the Winchester to empty the magazine. He hurled the empty rifle far into the dark brush. He picked up his own rifle and swung up into the saddle. "I work alone," he said quietly.

"I'll report you to Sheriff Luscombe!" cried Beatty.

"Please do," politely suggested Lee. "And, while you're at it, *manhunter,* you tell him how Chad Mercer outsmarted you, taking four horses away from four big men. You call yourself a manhunter, Beatty? Go on back to Cibola on foot and turn in your badge or stick to issuing dog licenses and throwing drunks out of the whorehouses that give you a cut for the service rendered." He touched the chestnut with his heels and rode down the draw, leading the dun.

"I hope to Christ Mercer turns on you and kills you, Kershaw!" roared Beatty.

Lee looked back at him. "I can do a little killing myself," he said. He rode south beyond the mouth of the draw. There was a faint touch of pale gray appearing over the dark serrated rim of the San Mateos. The wind had died. When Lee was half a mile from the draw, he pulled out a brandy bottle and took a stiff pull from it. He wiped his mouth with the back of a hand. "Bastards," he said. He grinned as the chestnut bobbed his head in full agreement.

FOUR

THE CHESTNUT WAS worn out by the time Lee could look down the long heat-hazed slopes to where a far-distant line of dark and dusty willows marked the course of the Rio Grande to the east. Across the river were the Fra Cristobal Mountains shimmering lazily in the rising heat waves. Farther south was the dim line of the Caballo Mountains. Lee turned in the saddle and looked up the slopes toward the west. He had a feeling he was being followed. He hadn't seen anyone, but the persistent feeling was within him that there was someone behind him hidden in the broken folds of the foothills and that perhaps even now he was being watched.

He rode slowly down the long slope. Behind him across the southern end of the Black Range was Silver City. To his right down the long Rio Grande Valley, eighty miles away, was Las Cruces with El Paso forty miles to the south, on the Chihuahua border. Just across the river was the State of Chihuahua—and Lopez, most likely. It wasn't likely Mercer would have followed the river road on the west side of the Rio Grande. He might run into a posse riding east from Silver City or north from Las Cruces. Bennett Luscombe's telegraph messages had by now alerted all of southern New Mexico Territory to the fact that Mercer was trying for Chihuahua.

Lee reached the rutted road and sat the tired chestnut while scanning the terrain to the south, east, and north. "Upriver, I'll bet," he said aloud. "The slick sonofabitch. He'd be able to cross the Rio Grande at Valverde Crossing." He touched the horse with his heels. The chestnut stumbled in its weariness. Lee passed a hand along its sweating neck. "Just a little while longer, amigo," he promised.

The sun was low over the western mountains when Lee saw the little estancia held in a fold of the ground between Lee and the river bottoms. Lee dismounted and took out his field glasses to focus them on the heat-shimmering slopes west of the valley road. A thin wraith of dust was rising. "Two horsemen," mused Lee thoughtfully. He mounted and rode toward the estancia.

A sombreroed man watched Lee from beside a corral. He smiled as he recognized Lee. "Señor Kershaw!" he cried. "A pleasure to see you. You are perhaps looking for your compañero Señor Mercer, eh?"

"You know it, José," replied Lee as he dismounted. "You have gained the weight, my friend."

"I got married since the last time I saw you," said José proudly.

"Well, we can't always win," Lee said. "Where is the Señor Mercer?" He rested his hand against his gun belt just above his holstered Colt.

"He rode to the Valverde Crossing after he traded horses with me," replied José. "That was early this morning. He got from me a roan and a claybank. But he did not say he expected you, Señor Kershaw."

Lee smiled. "Oh, he knows it all right," said Lee. "Did he, by any chance, say where he was going?"

José hesitated. "He said he was heading for the Pecos."

"Across two hundred miles of the Jornado and the Lava Flow in this heat? There's no water out there either."

"It did sound strange to me," admitted José. He eyed Lee. "He was in the big hurry."

Lee unsaddled the chestnut and saddled the dun. He led both horses to the watering trough and while they drank he filled his canteens.

José cleared his throat. "What has he done?" he asked.

Lee glanced casually at the New Mexican. "Horse thieving," he replied.

José paled a little. He glanced nervously at his corral.

"Those horses have the Rolling L brand, eh, amigo?" asked Lee.

"That is so," admitted José.

"Do you know whose brand that is?"

José smiled weakly. "No, I cannot say that I do."

"Bennett Luscombe's brand," explained Lee.

José paled again. "Mother of God!" he cried.

"I can arrange it so that you may keep those horses, Joselito, my friend."

José glanced toward the river. "I do not like to say anything about Señor Mercer," he said huskily. He looked back into Lee's cold blue Yanqui eyes. José pointed south. "He crossed the river at Valverde. He told me to tell anyone who asked about him that he had crossed the

29

Jornado and the Lava Flow, heading for the Pecos River. It is in my mind that he really intended to ride south on the Jornado del Muerto."

Lee nodded. "Ninety waterless miles in this heat."

José shrugged. "Except for perhaps Ojo del Muerte. It may not be dry. If he is desperate, he may risk it."

Lee shaped a cigarette and handed the tobacco canteen to José. Lee lighted up and looked south along the line of the Rio Grande Valley. "Ojo del Muerte," he mused, almost as though to himself. "The Eye of Death. Any Apache trouble there lately?"

"A few Mescaleroes, no more, my friend. They stole mules from the soldiers this spring."

"There are soldiers there now?"

"None," replied José as he fashioned a cigarette.

Lee lighted José's cigarette. He looked beyond the man and saw faint drifting dust on the hazy slopes beyond the valley road. "There will be someone here asking about me," he said quietly. "Drive those Rolling L horses into the bottoms and picket them there. Play stupid, my friend."

"I am very good at that, Señor Kershaw!" cried José.

"It's not really out of character," murmured Lee in English. He handed José a ten-dollar bill. José whistled softly. Lee took José gently by the lapels of his jacket and drew him close. "Now, my little friend," he said in a low voice, "one must listen, and listen well. Do not worry about the Rolling L brand on those horses. I can arrange it so that there is no trouble about them. In exchange, one must keep one's big mouth shut if I am followed here. Understand?"

José nodded. "Upon my word of honor!" he cried.

Lee mounted the dun and led the chestnut toward the river bottoms, riding slowly so as not to raise the dust. He kept to the low ground and in among the dusty brush and willows until it was dusk and he reined in at the edge of the wide and shallow Valverde Crossing. He unsheathed his rifle and held it above his head as he rode splashing across the river. He kept his eyes on the dark line of the eastern bank, with the uneasy feeling in the back of his mind that Chad Mercer might very well be waiting there in ambush, already eyeing Lee over the buckhorn sights of his rifle.

Lee reached the east bank and led the horses into a *bosquecillo* of cottonwoods. He tethered them there and took his rifle. He padded softly across the open ground to another *bosquecillo* to look toward the open ground that sloped down toward the darkened surface of the murmuring river. A dry and fitful breeze stirred the leaves of the trees and rustled the brush. Nothing moved. Lee went back for the horses and led them across the open ground. Something rolled beneath his left boot sole. He picked up a flattened minie ball. There were many of them scattered over the area. Lee was crossing Valverde, where a battle was fought in 1862 between the Texans of Sibley's Brigade and the Union force of Regulars from Fort Craig across the river and the New Mexico Volunteers. The battle had been fought for possession of the all-important ford known as Valverdes' Crossing. Lee's father had fought there with the First New Mexico Volunteers under the command of Colonel Kit Carson and as a result of the bloody encounter had carried a rebel minie ball in his left thigh for the remainder of his life.

Beyond the open ground were the few eroded ruins of what had once been Valverde, the "Green Valley," which had been a "King's axe" sanctuary for the rest and recuperation of travelers during the Spanish Colonial Period, for it had afforded good grazing for horses, mules, and oxen and good water for man and beast, as well as grateful shade from the many trees that had once, long past, filled much of the area. It had been a haven for the travelers from the south who had just crossed the dreaded Journey of Death that extended from the curving Rio Grande ninety miles south of Valverde and passing east of the Caballos and the Fra Cristobals.

Lee passed faded headboards, warped and split by the weather and with the names long worn away from the surfaces. Now and then he would look quickly back over one shoulder or the other. Valverde was an eerie, lonely place, seemingly forgotten by the living and haunted by the ghosts of those that had died there—Apaches, Spaniards, Mexicans, Texans, and New Mexicans.

Lee led the two horses into a draw at the southern side of the great bowl that was Valverde. There would be a moon later on. Lee foot-scouted up the draw looking for traces of Chad Mercer's passage but found none. He'd likely pick up trace beyond the cup of hills within which Valverde was sheltered.

The wind shifted and now came from the west. The faint sound of splashing came to Lee. Then the sound died away. Lee led the two horses further up the draw. The wind would bring the presence of other horses to his pair and he didn't want them making any welcoming noises. He took his rifle and walked down the draw and up the side of it to find a shallow place where he could survey the area and yet not be seen himself. Minutes ticked slowly past. A faint wash of moonlight appeared in the eastern sky. A horse whinnied near the crossing, on the Valverde side of the Rio Grande. The faint sound of voices came to Lee. In a little while he heard the soft thudding of hoof falls on the sandy ground. Something moved near the ancient adobes. A voice sounded again. A quick spurt of light showed through the window of an adobe.

Lee bellied along the ground toward the adobe. A horse blew in the darkness. Light flickered up within the adobe and the sound of fire crackling wood came to Lee with the resinous odor of burning. Someone passed between the firelight and a window of the adobe. Voices sounded hollowly from within the small building. Two men, thought Lee.

The wind shifted to the south. It blew a little harder. One of the two horses near the adobe whinnied sharply and was instantly echoed by one of Lee's horses. He cursed softly as he slid down into the draw and ran toward his two mounts. Lee reached the dun. The chestnut tossed his head and whinnied. "Shut up, damn you!" grated Lee.

"Don't move," the voice said from the darkness on the north rim of the deep draw. "Get away from those horses!

32

Drop that rifle! Pronto!" The voice sounded familiar to Lee. He dropped the rifle and stepped back from the dun. "Drop that gun belt!" came the command. Lee slowly unbuckled the gun belt and let it drop to the ground. He raised his arms. "Get up here!" was the next order. Lee obediently slogged up the side of the draw. The faint light of the rising moon revealed a man standing behind a dying cottonwood with a rifle in his hands. "Walk toward that adobe!" he ordered. Lee glanced sideways at the man as he passed the cottonwood. "Howdy, young fella," he said amiably. "You're a long way from Cibola, Gil. What's the game? Cowboys and Indians?"

"Keep moving!" snapped Gil. "Get inside that adobe!"

Lee walked into the firelighted adobe and opened his eyes a little wider. A young woman stood beside the beehive fireplace with a rifle in her slim hands. Her titian-colored hair hung down her back in two thick braids. Her great green eyes studied Lee. Lee whistled softly. A gun muzzle jabbed hard just over his kidneys. "It was easy, Leila," boasted the kid. "Kershaw looked just like a kid stealing apples when I got the drop on him. Lee Kershaw! The man that can out-Indian an Apache! The big, tough manhunter!"

"Your little brother has a big mouth," observed Lee to Leila Luscombe.

"He did get the drop on you, didn't he?" she asked sweetly.

"Stand in the corner," commanded Gil.

He was like a kid with a new toy, thought Lee. He walked into the corner and rested his hands atop his hat. "You know you're both interfering with an officer of the law in the performance of his duty," he warned, feeling like he was parroting Morgan Beatty, and feeling damned silly as he did so. He looked sideways at the fireplace. "I'll have a plate of those beans," he suggested.

"Where's Chad Mercer?" demanded Leila.

Lee slanted his eyes at her. She looked better all the time. "That's what I'd like to know, ma'am," he replied.

"Did he cross the Rio Grande?" she asked.

"Probably," answered Lee.

"Where is he now?" she asked.

He shrugged. "Probably bustin' the wind heading south on the Jornado. Let's cut out this tomfoolery, eat some of those Mexican strawberries you're baking in that bean pot, and let me get on with my job. He's moving fast, ma'am!"

She shook her head. "You're staying right here with us, mister, until Chad reaches Mexico."

Lee narrowed his eyes. He looked back over his shoulder at Gil. "What the hell *is* this?" he asked. "You know your father deputized me and gave me a warrant for Mercer's arrest. Weren't you supposed to have gone to Cibola to send those wires your father ordered you to send?"

Gil grinned. "That's what he *thought* I was going to do, Kershaw."

Lee eyed the grinning kid. "You're a little too big for pranks," he said.

Gil shook his head. "No pranks," he said. "It's a bigger game than you figured on, mister. You've been outsmarted at your own game, Kershaw."

Lee looked at the woman. "Mercer murdered Frank," he said. "Every minute he's putting more ground behind him. If Gil didn't send those telegrams, chances are Mercer will be beyond reach by the time your father finds out what Gil has done."

Leila leaned her rifle in the corner beside the fireplace and knelt to stir the beans. "Chad Mercer did not kill my brother Frank," she said quietly.

"Your father thinks he did," said Lee.

"He wouldn't believe it if Frank came back from the grave to tell him," she said bitterly.

Lee looked with bewilderment from her to Gil and then back to her again. "This is loco," he said slowly. "What's your game?"

Gil grinned again. He was like a damned Cheshire Cat, thought Lee. Something came back to him—the night he had left his estancia he had heard hoofbeats on the valley road; two horses being ridden hard through the darkness to the south where no one lived. He had a damned good idea now who those two riders had been. "You followed me through the San Mateos," said Lee. "It was you who tailed me to the Rio Grande Valley."

"You thought you had thrown us off back there," jeered Gil. "I was too smart to fall for that."

"Do tell," murmured Lee. "How much did you pay José to have him tell you I had passed that way on my way to Valverde Crossing?"

"Not a peso," replied Gil. "I scouted the place before we rode up to it. I just happened to find some tired-out Rolling L horses picketed in the bottoms. I told José who we were and flashed my deputy's star on him. You should have seen the look on his face."

Lee nodded. "How old are you, Gil?" he asked.

"Eighteen, going on nineteen."

"You'll be a man before your sister," murmured Lee.

"I was man enough to catch Lee Kershaw!" retorted Gil.

Lee shook his head. "I didn't mean that," he said. "You were sworn in as a deputy by your father and you disobeyed his orders. You used that star illegally. You know what that means? You damned idiot! You can be jailed for what you've done!"

"It was my father who swore me in," reminded Gil.

"It was the *county sheriff* who swore you in," corrected Lee. "He can't change the law, sonny."

Gil grinned. "*My* pa can."

Lee nodeed. "You're maybe right at that. Why stop me from trying to catch Mercer?"

Gil jerked his head toward Leila. "Look at my sister," he suggested.

Lee looked at her and swift knowledge came to him. "So that's it! Does your father know about this?"

Gil nodded. "We think that's why my father suddenly tried to hang Frank's murder on Chad."

"So you rode as a deputy to see what your father planned to do and all the time your sister was waiting outside of my estancia for you to come and tell her."

Gil nodded again. "We weren't sure Dad would hire you to track down Chad. When we knew that, we figured we'd better give Chad a hand."

"To what end?" asked Lee.

Leila looked at Gil. "Chad has a rancho down in Chihuahua," she said quietly. "We plan to meet him there."

Lee laughed softly. "Christamighty!" he said. "I've heard the limit now!"

"We've stopped *you* at least," said Gil. He grinned at his lovely sister.

"Those Mexican strawberries are scorching, ma'am," said Lee.

Gil quickly turned his head to look at the bean pot. Lee closed his left hand on the brim of his Stetson and whirled to his left, slashing the heavy hat across the kid's startled face. He clamped his right hand on the kid's rifle barrel and jerked it from his big hands. Leila reached for her rifle. Gil recovered swiftly enough to kick out, knocking his rifle from Lee's hands. Gil cocked a big right fist and suddenly found himself looking right into the twin over-and-under muzzles of a double-barrelled derringer. "Step back like a little gentleman," politely suggested Lee.

"Where'd that stingy gun come from?" demanded Gil.

"Get back, damn you!" snapped Lee.

Gil was young enough and foolish enough to swing from the hip. Lee could have killed him then and there, but it wasn't in him, and likely the kid had at least figured out that gamble. Lee swayed back with the kid's wild punch. A looping left grazed Lee's right ear. Lee dropped the stingy gun into a pocket, swayed easily under a right cross, and came up with a left uppercut that snapped back Gil's head. He flung out his arms to hold his balance and Lee stepped in close with a perfectly timed one-two, belly and jaw, that dumped the kid back into a corner.

Lee had just time enough to jerk Leila's rifle from her hands and hurl it out of the closest window before the big boy was up on his feet and charging Lee like a blood-maddened bull. The very fury of his attack, unskilled as it was, was enough to smash Lee back against the wall and to make him take three blows that split his lower lip, cracked a molar, and brought the quick tears to his eyes.

Gil jumped back, jumping about like a trained bear, throwing experimental punches at thin air and grinning from ear to ear. "Come on, you tricky bastard!" he shouted.

"There's a lady present, sonny," Lee reminded as he came out from the wall with a probing left that straightened up the kid and a snapping right across that knocked him down on one knee. He came up fast with blood in his eye, snorting and puffing, but a hard knee caught him under the chin and a vicious backhander caught him across the eyes and dumped him back into the corner. Once he tried to raise his head, but a bootheel clipped him just behind the ear to keep him quietly floored.

"You could have killed him!" cried his sister.

Lee slowly wiped the blood from the side of his mouth and eyed her coldly. "He wasn't exactly playing pattycake with me, ma'am," he slowly replied. His breathing was harsh and all of a sudden he felt very tired. Too many hours in the saddle with no sleep and little food had drained his reserves more than he had realized. "Let me get this straight," he added. "Your father claims he has positive proof that Chad Mercer killed your brother Frank, and you two claim Chad is innocent and are willing to face a prison term to help him escape the law. You trailed me here all the way through the San Mateos to stop me from running down Chad. Do I have it right, ma'am?"

"You're getting the idea," she said truculently.

He leaned back against the wall and began to shape a cigarette. He lighted it and eyed her over the flare of the match. "It's really none of my business, Miss Luscombe, why you really want to help Chad Mercer and how you conned your baby brother into helping you, but don't try it again, with *me* at least. You understand?" He flipped the match into the fireplace. "You've cost me enough time as it is."

"You'll never catch him," she said quietly. "He's a better man than you are, Lee Kershaw."

"Then, why try to stop me?" he asked. He blew a smoke ring and watched it drift through a window. "After all, I'm only earning a honest buck in the line of work at which I am best fitted, according to your father, at least. Why stand in my way?"

She raised her head a little. "I hate your guts," she said in a low, flat voice. "Manhunter! You kill for money!"

He tapped his chest. "The warrant I carry here says Alive or Dead. Those are not *my* words, ma'am. I intend to bring Chad Mercer back alive."

"And dead if no other way!" she said.

He shook his head. "That's not my choice. It's his."

"You're like a machine," she accused.

"Once he's in your father's custody, my job is done," said Lee.

Her eyes seemed to strike at him. "How long do you think he'll live once my father and his so-called deputies get their hands on him?"

Lee shrugged. He walked to the door and turned to look back at her. "Now, when your baby brother gets up from his nap, he'll have a headache and a few other aches and pains. You feed him. He's a growing boy. In the morning he can cross the river and get two of those Rolling L horses from José."

"We've got horses, mister!" she snapped.

He grinned irritatingly. *"Had,"* he corrected. "Past tense, ma'am."

"You wouldn't!" she cried.

"Try me," he suggested. He glanced at Gil. "He'll be all right," he added. "The walk will do him good."

"No thanks to you!"

"I could say you're beautiful when you're angry, but right at this moment you look just like a redheaded woodpecker that just rammed his bill into a nail in a tree. Buenos noches, señorita!"

"You get to hell out of here!" she yelled.

He stuck his head in through a window. "That ain't very ladylike," he chided. He was gone before the pot of beans smashed against the wall beside the window. He pulled up the picket pins of their tired horses and led them to where he had left his two horses. He buckled on his gun belt and picked up his rifle. He swung up into the saddle.

"Wait! God damn you!" shouted Gil from the lip of the draw. The moonlight shone on his wild eyes and the bright blood that was still trickling down his face. His rifle was held tightly in his big hands.

Lee looked up at the kid, studying him for a second or two. Lee's rifle was across his thighs. "Listen mister," he said coldly. "I let you play out your little game back there. Now, don't try me again, sonny. I've had just about all I can stomach from you and your sister back there. *¿Comprende?*"

For a moment the big boy stood there, undecided, looking down at the cold-eyed man who sat his dun horse watching him, waiting for Gil to make his play. Gil wanted to try Lee Kershaw. God, how he wanted to try him! Lee touched the dun with his heels and rode up the far side of the draw leading the three horses. Gil did not move until Lee was out of sight. He turned and walked stiff-legged back toward the adobe with pure hell in his heart.

FIVE

THE MOONLIGHT GLISTENED from the rails of the Santa Fe, a long and silvery double line stretching from north to south on the dark and level ground of the Lava Flow following the old route of the Jornado del Muerte to meet the Rio Grande ninety miles to the south where the river curved toward the east. Lee dismounted and slapped the dusty rumps of the two Luscombe mounts and watched them as they trotted slowly back toward the hills that lay between the Lava Flow and the Rio Grande. They would head for the water and Gil and Leila would find them by morning. Lee made a cigarette. His ear still stung from Gil's wild blow. His lip was swollen and his mouth still tasted of blood. Would Bennett Luscombe know by now where his son and daughter had gone? Did he know *why* they had left Cibola?

Lee mounted the dun and rode across the railroad tracks, scouting for signs but hardly expecting to see any on that hard surface. He eyed the eastern mountains. There was a gap between the Sierra Oscura and the San Andres and beyond the gap was the *poblado* of Tularosa within the Tularosa Valley, which stretched one hundred and seventy-five miles south and west. Lee shook his head. He looked south along the railroad line to where the Jornado del Muerte stretched whitely under the moonlight beyond the dark Lava Flow. There was no sign of life out there. The wind had died. The creosote bushes and the palmitos stood stiffly still in the lunarlike landscape. There was not enough cover to conceal two horses and a man. Lee rode south. The horse's hoofs rang on the hard ground. Now and then Lee would look behind himself to the north. The land was as empty of life as the moon.

The moon was well on the wane and the hollows on the eastern flank of the Fra Cristobals were inking into shadows when Lee suddenly reined in the dun. He swung down and squatted in front of a pile of horse droppings. He raked his fingers through the pile. There was dampness within the pile. He crumbled some of the manure between his fingers. "Oats," he said aloud. He stood up and looked to the east. The railroad line was three miles that way. Lee had angled away from it on his route toward Ojo del Muerte. He led the dun and the chestnut on toward the spring. A mile further on he found a crushed cigarette butt. He broke it up in his fingers. "Fresh," he said. "Still southerly. He'll need water for tomorrow. He'll have to get it at Ojo del Muerte, *if* there's any there."

Lee chanced it. He mounted the dun and rode him hard toward the southwest and the dim notch in the mountains that marked Ojo del Muerte, The Eye of Death.

The spring was the only one on the eastern side of the Caballos and the Fra Cristobals for the ninety miles of the Jornado del Muerte. The moon waned and died as he rode on. He kept on through the thick, postmoon darkness, guiding himself by the outline of the notch. Just as the first traces of pewter dawn light showed in the eastern sky he dismounted and drew his Winchester from its scabbard. The wind began to rise with the coming of the dawn, swaying the dark brush and pushing fine, loose gravel across the hard-surfaced caliche. Lee took out rawhide boots from a saddlebag and put them on the two horses. He led them on again. The ground surface changed into hummocks wigged with coarse and lifeless-looking brush.

The dawn light was at Lee's back. He glanced behind him. At that instant a rifle crashed somewhere up on the rising slopes between Lee and the spring. The chestnut went down and lay still and the dun jerked the reins from Lee's hand and galloped to the east toward the distant railway line. The rifle cracked again and the slug whipped past Lee's head. Lee hit the ground behind a hummock and shoved forward his rifle even as he levered a round into the chamber. By God, he thought, Mescaleroes! He touched his dry, swollen lips with the tip of his tongue.

Minutes dragged past. Lee bellied along the harsh ground, cursing mentally as flinty shards ripped through his clothing and cut his flesh. Foot by foot he silently worked his way up the slope to flank the spring. He took off his hat and left it behind as he squirmed up the reverse slope of a low ridge. Just as the sun tipped the San Andres, Lee peered down into the great hollow wherein lay Ojo del Muerte. There was no sign of life down there. Further to his right, on a level area, were the abandoned ruins of little Fort McRae that had been built there by the California Volunteers during the Civil War to protect the spring from the Mescaleroes and Mimbres Apaches. The empty windows stared back at Lee like eye sockets in a skull.

Lee waited as the sun rose. It was quiet except for the gravelly whispering of the wind. He slid back down the slope and got his hat, then walked at a swift crouching pace to the place from which the rifle had been fired. He found two fresh brass hulls glinting in the morning sunlight. They were .44/40 cases. The earth was disturbed. Lee kicked at it. The corner of a gray blanket showed. He tugged it free from the loose earth. Dirt pattered down into a hole beneath the blanket. Several cigarette butts lay in the rifle pit. There were knee and elbow holes where the hidden rifleman had taken careful aim to down the chestnut. A man could have walked right up to that hole without seeing anyone until it was too late.

Lee walked up the slope. The growing sunlight showed that the fort was empty of life. Lee found some water in a shallow *tinaja*. He lay bellyflat and pushed back the greenish float and a few pinkish bladders. He sipped a little water. "Coyote tea," he said as he sat up and wiped his swollen mouth. He walked up the slope to the fort. The rising wind rolled a tumbleweed across the quadrangle between the eroded buildings.

In the third building Lee entered he found fresh ashes in a fireplace and the fieldstone hearth beneath them was still warm. Several cigarette butts still lay about. An empty brandy bottle lay to one side with some empty and unrusted tin cans. Lee read the label on one of the cans: "Sweetheart Brand Choice Peas." He eyed the brandy bottle. It was Jerez brandy. He walked outside and looked to the west up the broken slopes and to the narrow, precipitous gap that led to the western side of the mountains, beyond which was the Rio Grande. He walked up toward the gap and found faint tracks and a frayed and badly worn rawhide horse boot.

A horse whinnied down near the spring and Lee faded into the brush. He looked down to see his dun standing at the *tinaja* drinking the remaining water. The faint and far-off whistling of a locomotive came to Lee on the wind that was sweeping from the north. A thin feather of wind-driven smoke was rising out on the Jornado. Lee plunged down the slope and mounted the dun. He rode hard down the remaining slope and let the dun run loose for the railroad line. When he reached the rail line, he had time for one cigarette by the time the freight train was within a quarter of a mile of him. He kneed the dun up on the right of way and in between the rails, then stood up in his stirrups and waved his hat. The train slowed down. A head was thrust out of each side of the locomotive cab. Two men ran along the tops of the freight cars carrying rifles as the train ground to a shuddering halt fifty yards from Lee.

"What the hell do you want?" a truculent voice yelled from the locomotive. "We're twenty minutes late as it is!"

Lee rode toward the locomotive flashing his star as he did so. "Deputy-Sheriff Lee Kershaw," he said. "I'm trailing a man wanted for murder. I think he's gone over the Fra Cristobals and will head south along the Rio Grande Valley. I want a ride as far south as Las Cruces."

"Joe," said the engineer to the conductor. "We can load that dun onto that empty flat. Let's get cracking. I can make up my time between here and the Rio."

In ten minutes the dun was on the flat car and the train was slowly gathering speed. In twenty more minutes Lee had finished a plate of ham and eggs. In half an hour he was sound asleep in one of the crummy's bunks.

SIX

LEE KERSHAW LEANED against the counter in the Las Cruces telegraph office and fashioned a cigarette. "Read that copy list aloud to me," he said to the clerk.

The clerk scanned the list. "Copies to be sent to Sheriff Bennett Luscombe at Cibola, the Frontier Battalion of the Texas Rangers at Ysleta, the El Paso Police, copies, one each, to the sheriffs of Luna, Hidalgo, Doña Ana, Sierra, and Otero counties, all in the Territory of New Mexico.

43

Copies to the railroad police of both the Southern Pacific and the Santa Fe railroads. Copies to the sheriffs of Cochise, Graham, and Santa Cruz counties in Arizona Territory. A copy to the police of Ciudad Juarez, State of Chihuahua, Mexico, with a request added to it that the information contained in the message be forwarded to the Local Commandant of the Rurales." The clerk looked up at Lee. "All of these copies to be signed by your name, Mr. Kershaw?"

Lee nodded. "With the exception of the wire to the Juarez Police and the Rurales. Sign that with the name of Sheriff Bennett Luscombe."

The clerk eyed Lee quickly and then looked quickly away from Lee's steady look. Lee lighted his cigarette.

"You're spreading quite a net for this man Chad Mercer," commented the clerk.

Lee smiled. "Saves time and a lot of hard riding," he said. "Trouble is, it should have been done two days ago."

The door of the telegraph office was opened and a touseled head was thrust in. "Your dun is ready, mister," said the boy. "He has new shoes and I fed and watered him myself."

"Gracias," said Lee. He tossed the kid a coin.

"Por nada, señor," replied the boy.

Lee paid for the telegraph messages and left the office. He walked through the bright midday sunshine to the livery stable to get his dun. Odds were that the telegraph messages were in time, with the exception of the one to Silver City—the crucial one that Gil Luscombe was responsible for and which he had not sent. The dun had rested some during his train ride. Lee paid the blacksmith and led the dun to a general store, where Lee replenished his food supplies, tobacco, and brandy. He stowed the supplies in his saddlebags under the watchful eyes of the boy. "Do you remember well, muchacho?" asked Lee.

"I know the man from your description, señor," replied the boy. "I will know him if I see him."

"Tell me of him," requested Lee.

"He is as tall as you. A younger man than you with blond hair and mustache and with gray eyes. He smiles a

44

lot with his face but not always with his eyes and he has the so beautiful teeth."

"Bueno!" said Lee. He mounted the dun and looked down at the boy. "If you see such a man, tell the police at once." He tossed the kid a coin and touched the dun with his heels. Lee rode to the west and out of the town. He reined in the dun at a crossroads and shaped and lighted a cigarette as he scanned the open country. Mercer would be heading in a southerly direction along the valley of the Rio Grande, but he'd have to stay off the good valley road and make his way through rougher going. He would be tired by now and would need some rest. His mounts would need rest as well. He could not afford to lose them. "He'll hole up somewhere," said Lee thoughtfully. "He can drive his horses to death and he can go without food, but neither he nor his horses can stand such a pace in this heat without water." He touched the dun with his heels and rode on toward the west.

The southbound afternoon combination had pulled into Las Cruces and the tender was being watered. Leila Luscombe stood beside the train looking down the dusty street for her brother.

"We're leaving in three minutes, ma'am," said the conductor to Leila. He eyed her appreciatively. She wore a split corduroy riding skirt, figured boots, a light flannel shirt, and an open leather jacket. Her wide-brimmed hat hung by its strap at the back of her neck. "Best get aboard," added the conductor. "I'll give you a hand with your saddles and gear."

"I'm waiting for my brother," she replied. She walked to the edge of the platform and saw Gil running toward the station. Gil pointed to the train and shook his head.

"All aboard!" cried the conductor. "You coming along, ma'am?"

Leila shook her head. Gil panted up to the edge of the platform. He shoved back his hat and wiped the sweat from his forehead. "He was here all right," he reported. "A kid told me he came in on a freight train early this morning and had his dun shoed. He sent a lot of telegraph messages and then left town after buying supplies. He headed west out of town on the Deming Road."

Leila was puzzled. "Why west, Gil? Chad was on the east side of the Rio Grande. Why would he have crossed back to the west side of it?"

Gil grinned. "Chad was smart enough to slip back across the Rio Grande, figuring Kershaw was looking for him on the *east* side."

She shook her head and looked west. "Chad took an awful risk. By this time every lawman west of the Rio Grande between the San Mateos and the Chihuahua border has been alerted by Lee Kershaw, if they haven't already been alerted by Dad sending wires from Cibola."

Gil picked up the two saddles and slung one each over a shoulder. "They haven't caught him yet," he said.

"Maybe he's heading for Arizona," she suggested.

He shrugged. "Only if he can't get to the border from New Mexico Territory. Chad's only chance now is to head south on the west side of the Rio Grande. There's a lot of empty country west of here, sis."

"And no water to speak of," she added.

"He'll have to risk that."

"They'll be watching all the waterholes."

"Chad knows that! But once he gets across the border, he knows Kershaw won't dare follow him."

Leila picked up their sheathed rifles and other gear. "Are you sure about that?" she asked.

Gil nodded. "Badge or no badge; warrant or no warrant, the Rurales and Federals know Lee Kershaw as one of the gunfighting Yanquis who has fought for Lopez a few times. There's a death sentence hanging over his head once he steps across the Mex border. They won't waste any time with him, I tell you! *Ley del fuego!* They'll give him a two-minute start on foot and then start shooting, and they won't miss."

"You could say the same thing about Chad, Gil," she reminded him.

"Don't worry about Chad. If he gets across the border he'll join Lopez and the Rurales and Federales would have to defeat Lopez to get Chad. Even if Kershaw does follow Chad across the border, he'll have to keep out of the sight of the lawmen down there. If Chad reaches Lopez and tells him Kershaw has crossed the border wearing a Yanqui badge and with a Yanqui warrant for Chad in his pocket, that will queer Kershaw with Lopez, I tell you!"

She nodded. "Which means that every man's hand will be against Lee Kershaw once he crosses into Mexico." She looked to the west as she followed Chad down the dusty street. "It seems awfully cruel, Gil."

He turned and looked at her. "Look, sis! It's Kershaw or Chad in this game. Dead or alive! And you can take that either way. There won't be any other way for those two. You'd better get that through your head right now! Kershaw might capture Chad, but he'll never get him back to Cibola alive. Another thing: I'm already in trouble because I did not send those telegrams from Cibola. I've aided and abetted a man who is escaping from the law, whether or not he's innocent. I tried to stop Kershaw back at Valverde and you helped me. If we go on like this, trying to help Chad escape, and he *does* escape, you know what that means?"

She nodded. "We won't be able to come back to New Mexico if we go into Mexico. If we do, we'll face a trial and a prison term."

"You've got it," said her brother. "Another thing: If we do reach Chad in Mexico, you'll be living with a man who is known throughout Chihuahua and Sonora as a *revolutionario*. He can be shot on sight."

She stared at her brother. "But his ranch? Won't we be safe if we live on his ranch?"

"Only if he does not join Lopez and can get a pardon from the Mexican government."

She hesitated. "I never really thought of that, Gil."

"You'd better think about it right now. I'm in deep in this thing, but you're still in the clear. You haven't really done anything."

"I helped you against Lee Kershaw," she reminded him.

"I don't believe he'd press charges against you."

"But what about you?"

Gil grinned. "You know it!" he replied. He studied her for a moment. "You know the rules of the game we're playing. It's not too late for you to quit. Is this what you really want? Make up your mind right now."

She looked toward the west, where Chad Mercer was likely holed up in the enervating heat of the day, probably without food and water, waiting his chance to slip across the border into Mexico through a tightening net of hard-eyed lawmen and with one of the greatest, if not the greatest, manhunters in the Southwest after him, bearing a warrant that read "Dead or Alive." "We'll need horses, water, and supplies," she said quietly. "I'll get the supplies."

He nodded. "There will be no going back," he reminded her.

She walked on down the dusty street.

Within an hour Gil had bought a blocky bay for himself and a slim-flanked roan mare for his sister. Leila had purchased supplies from the same general store where Lee Kershaw had recently been.

Gil tightened the saddle cinch on the roan mare and then turned to look at his sister. "It's gettin' on," he said quietly. "We'll have to ride fast, sis."

She nodded. They mounted and rode west on the Deming Road as the sun tilted low over the western mountains.

SEVEN

THE SWIFT AND TINY spurt of light came through the velvety darkness like bright sunlight reflecting suddenly from the facet of a diamond, and then it was gone.

Lee turned the dun to cross the Southern Pacific tracks. An indistinct sound came on the night wind. Again he saw that swift splash of light, as though someone had drawn in hard on a cigarette. Lee glanced at the eastern sky. There would be a moon later on. Chad Mercer would have to make his bid for the border before that time. He'd likely try to get across the Southern Pacific tracks before moonrise and then head for the lonely and isolated West Potrillo Mountains, or perhaps the Floridas.

A horse neighed in the darkness and the sound was windborne to Lee. He dismounted and drew his Winchester from its scabbard. Something grated on the harsh ground. "Stand where you are!" came the sudden warning out of the darkness. Lee went low and skylighted four mounted men. "This is the law!" shouted one of the horsemen. "Deputy-Sheriff Luna County! Stand where you are!"

"Lee Kershaw!" called out Lee. "That sounds like Bert Dixon."

"It is, Lee!" yelled back Dixon. "What the hell are you doing this far south?" He laughed. "You fly down here?"

"Keep your voice down," cautioned Lee as they rode toward him. "The wind carries the sound too damned well."

The four possemen dismounted and Bert Dixon stuck out a hand. "Good to see you back in harness," he said heartily. "Where's Chad Mercer, eh? You damned old bloodhound! You should know!"

"He must have crossed the Rio Grande sometime early this morning somewhere north of here," replied Lee.

"We've got a chance to net him, then," said Dixon.

Lee shook his head. "He's got two horses and he's likely already ridden one of them to death. He won't waste any time."

Dixon nodded. "We got a wire from Cibola yesterday. Sheriff Luscombe sent it. His information was that Mercer was in the San Mateos and that Morgan Beatty was hot on his trail and that you were riding solo after him. I still think he's east of the Rio Grande heading for the Panhandle."

Lee looked past the lawman. "Put out that cigarette," he said to one of the possemen.

"Who the hell are you to tell me that?" demanded the man.

"That light can be seen for better than a mile," said Lee.

"Listen to him!" jeered the posseman.

Dixon looked back over his shoulder. "Kershaw is right, Joe," he said. "Kill that butt."

Lee leaned back against his dun and cut a chew of Wedding Cake. "Mercer was at the spring at Ojo del Muerte this morning at dawn. He dropped one of my horses with a rifle bullet and then splitassed through the gap west to the Rio Grande. He likely crossed the Rio Grande early this morning and started to work his way south beyond the valley road."

"How'd you get here so fast?" asked Dixon, curious.

"Flagged down a Santa Fe freight and rode into Las Cruces," replied Lee as he stuffed the chew into his mouth.

"Smart," said Dixon. "We've got men strung out all along the railroad line and posses patrolling like we are."

"He won't head east again," said Lee. He shifted his chew and spat. He looked sideways at Dixon. "Why all this sudden interest in Chad Mercer?"

Dixon waved a hand. "Luna County is always glad to cooperate, Lee," he replied.

"Bullshit!" said Lee easily. "How much reward did Luscombe offer for Mercer?"

"Five thousand, dead or alive," replied Dixon. "Is Luscombe *that* serious about Mercer?"

Lee nodded. "He can back that reward."

"Dead or alive," said Bert. He slapped his rifle butt. "That always makes it easier." He eyed Lee curiously. "How'd you get in on this? Word was that you'd gone back to your grandpappy's old estancia in the Querencia and was ranching instead of manhunting. Besides, wasn't Chad Mercer your best friend?"

"Was," said Lee dryly.

"I guess that five thousand reward was enough to get

50

you off that ranch even if Mercer was your best friend, eh, Kershaw?" asked one of the men.

Lee caught the bite in the man's tone. "I just now learned about the five thousand," he said.

Joe spat sideways. "They say your manhunting rates was always high anyways," he remarked.

Dixon turned. "Lee is the best pro in the business!"

"Which means he'll get that five thousand before we do," said Joe.

Lee shook his head. "I'm not in on that," he said quietly. "I get my fee. That's all I want."

Dixon tilted his head to one side. "You sure, Lee?"

Lee ignored him. "While we're standing around here jawing, Mercer could slip past us."

"Any suggestions?" asked Bert.

"Spread your men out along the railroad within earshot of a rifle. You ride around like you've been doing and a deaf man could have seen you and maybe even heard you. Spread out, stand still, be quiet, and wait until one of you spots him. Then fire three times. The rest of you ought to be able to close in on him before he can get very far. His horses, or horse, should be worn thin about now and he won't be in any great shape himself."

"He's like spring steel and whang leather," growled one of the men. "Ain't no one can wear out Chad Mercer."

"Is he dangerous, Kershaw?" asked the oldest of the three possemen.

"It's Chad Mercer you're hunting," replied Lee quietly. He said nothing more as he mounted his dun. "Where's the closest water?" he asked.

"Ten miles due, south," replied Dixon. "But Mercer must still be north of us, Lee."

"What's south of here?" asked Lee.

"Low hills with lots of open country in between. Little cover. When the moonlight hits out there, anyone riding across those flats will look as though he's on a stage behind footlights."

"Where's the waterhole?"

"Due south, like I said. It's an old stagecoach swing station. The old Southern Overland Mail line ran through

51

there before the war. The place has been abandoned for about twenty-five years since they found water here along the line of the S.P. We've got all the water holes along the S.P. line covered by our men."

Lee nodded. He rode south and when out of sight of the possemen, he let the dun go at an easy run until he reached the faint ruts of an old road that curved to the southwest around a range of low hills. He followed the road through the darkness until he reached a deep arroyo. He stood up in his stirrups and something caught his eye beyond the arroyo. It was a darker thickness that must be an old building of some sort or another.

Lee led the dun down into the arroyo and tethered it to some scrub brush. He took out a pair of *n'deh b'keh* Apache desert moccasins and pulled off his boots, wincing a little as his well-used socks perfumed the night air. He pulled on the desert mocs and folded the thigh parts down below his knees and thonged them in place. He hung his hat on the saddlehorn, sipped a little water, then took his rifle and padded silently along the arroyo until he could see the road. Beyond the road was the building and behind it were the ruins of what had once been a large walled corral. There was a faint pewter trace of moonlight in the eastern sky. He circled the ruins widely and came in from the south side. The moon was up now and the light reflected dully from the leaden-colored surface of the spring-fed *tinaja* beside the swing station. Lee went to ground and bellied through the brush until he could overlook the *tinaja*. He scanned the ground about the waterhole. The growing moonlight revealed several large stones that had been disturbed; their heavier and darker sides were uppermost, indicating they had been likely upset by boots and hooves.

Lee belly-scouted along the harsh ground, looking for trace. The moon was fully up when he figured out that one man and two horses had been in the area within hours. Lee crawled into a gravelly hollow and watched the ruins. A faint puff of smoke drifted from one of the windows. The wind shifted a little and brought the smell of horses to Lee. Someone was holed up in the ruins and he had taken his mounts in there with him. It must be Chad Mercer and yet it was hard to believe that it was. He must have moved constantly to cross the S.P. tracks before they were guarded, or perhaps he had slipped across them between patrols. Either way, he had ridden like a Comanche that day through a burning hell of sun and most likely without water.

Lee squatted in the brush. "Smart," he said softly. Mercer had reached the ruins long before it would have been anticipated he would have gotten that far south. He had watered himself and his horses and was now resting, sitting it out until the moon waned and died and men hunted for him along the S.P. line ten miles to the north. When the moon was gone, he'd make his try for the border.

The moon rose higher and shadows gathered on the western side of the ruins. The wind shifted and increased, scrabbling softly over the harsh earth and moaning a little about the ruins. Time dragged. Lee did not move. Only his eyes and his jaws moved. At intervals he'd spit and then wipe his mouth with the back of a hand, but he never took his eyes from the ruins.

The moon seemed stuck in the clear sky but at last it moved westward and then hung over the western hills. A shadow grew thicker in the wide doorway of the station. A man suddenly and quietly led a saddled horse into the open. The rawhide-booted hoofs thudded softly on the hard ground. The man led out a second horse, this one unsaddled. The second horse was nervous, tossing his head up and down and neighing softly. He was a talker. The wind was blowing toward Lee, so the horse could not have scented him, yet something was making him nervous.

Lee slid forward his rifle and settled the blade front sight within the arc of the buckhorn rear sight and then centered the sights on the man. Lee narrowed his eyes. As yet he could not identify the man. The man mounted the saddled horse. Lee quickly shifted the sights to the horse. It was risky and Lee still could not make sure the man was Mercer. Lee again shifted the sights, this time to the barebacked horse. Just as Lee touched off the Winchester the saddled horse threw his head sideways and the heavy .44/40 slug smashed into his brain and dropped him without a kick. The man had kicked free of the stirrups as he heard the rifle report and had landed lightly on his feet. He turned toward the second horse and his face was fully revealed in the moonlight. It *was* Chad Mercer!

Lee fired at the second horse just as it moved. The heavy slug smashed into the station wall and sang eerily off into space. The horse stampeded. Mercer dived through a window. The rolling echo of the shot died away and the powdersmoke drifted off on the wind, but by that time Lee was fifty feet away from the firing position. He fired through the window and moved again. "Go to ground, you sonofabitch," said Lee between his teeth. The dull hoofbeats of the stampeded horse died away.

The moon moved further west. Shadows began to grow thicker on the eastern side of the swing station. Lee bellied through the brush, getting closer to the station. A horse neighed sharply. Lee cursed. The stampeded horse was trotting toward the station and this one did not have on rawhide boots. For one awful moment Lee thought it was his own dun and then he recognized it as a light bay horse. He narrowed his eyes. Where the hell had *it* come from? Lee raised his head. Someone was calling to the bay. Boots grated on the ground. A shadow detached itself from the ruins and legged it toward the stray horse.

Lee snapped up his rifle. There was a splash of red flame to his right flank followed by the flat report of a rifle. The slug ricocheted from the hard earth a foot to one side of Lee and splattered the right side of his face with stinging gravel. Lee rolled into the wash, cursing as he went. A second slug whispered right over his head to keep him down. The hard tattoo of hoofs sounded from the south as Chad Mercer made his bid for the border. Lee risked it. He jumped to his feet and hit the ground again as the rifle flatted off and sent a slug whispering past his head.

Lee worked his way along the wash. Maybe his dun

was gone. Whoever was helping Mercer might have taken the dun. Lee risked a dash across the open and dived into cover as the rifle cracked. Minutes ticked slowly past. Lee at last raised his head.

"Hey, Kershaw!" yelled Gil Luscombe. "You *lose* something?" Raucous laughter followed the sound of the kid's voice and then hoofbeats hammered on the flats and faded away, leaving Lee standing there with his useless rifle in his hands and pure unadulterated hell in his heart.

EIGHT

LEE CATFOOTED DOWN the road, making little sound on the harsh earth except for the faint whispering of the hard soles of his moccasins. He reached the dun and ripped loose the reins from the brush. He flung himself up into the saddle and slapped the dun on the rump with the flat of the rifle's buttstock. He plunged the dun across the road and through the thorned brush, feeling the needles ripping at his legs. He stood up in the stirrups and saw dust boiling up out of an arroyo to his left and two hundred yards from the ruins. He drove the dun through the tangle of brush and down into the arroyo again in time to see a horseman trying to buck-jump his mount up the crumbling side of the arroyo. The horse slipped back and nearly went down sideways, but the rider got control and the horse made the try again and this time cleared the rim of the arroyo.

Lee set the dun at the bank and went up it in a scattering of gravel. The horseman was slashing south through the brush. Lee let the dun run free. Twice Lee raised his rifle and twice he lowered it. All he had to do was to shoot down Gil Luscombe by mistake; despite what the kid had done, his father would force Lee to make a break for the Mexican border as Chad had done.

The horseman cut hard to the right and went down into another arroyo and along it toward the west with Lee racing along on the level ground beside the arroyo and gaining every foot of the way. His quarry turned the horse hard left and the horse went down, sliding in the loose gravel and throwing its rider into the softer side of the embankment in the shadows. Lee plunged the dun down into the arroyo, kicked loose the stirrups, sheathed the Winchester, and then slid from the saddle to land cat-footed on the ground. In three strides he rushed the fallen man. They met face to face as the man got to his feet. The impact of Lee's charge carried them both back against the bank into a tangle of catclaw. A knee came up hard in Lee's gut and a hand clawed for his eyes. Lee fell sideways, dragging his opponent down on top of him and a long strand of thickly braided hair struck him across the face. His hard hands found softness where they should have met more muscular flesh. "For Christ's sake!" he yelled. *"You!"* He threw Leila Luscombe back down into the bottom of the arroyo.

She came to her feet, dragging at her holstered Colt. Lee swung sideways as he came up off the bank and caught her with a hard chop across the gun wrist as she drew. She dropped the pistol and as he closed in on her she raked both hands down the sides of his face and he felt the sting of her ripping nails. He swung up his left hand to behind his right ear and cut it hard, backhanding her alongside the head to knock her flat on her back. She struggled to get up, but he planted an easy boot on her right wrist and pressed it down. "Now, damn you!" he exploded. "Lie still or you'll get the other boot!"

She did not try to move again, but her great green eyes were like emerald fire as she looked up at him. A thin trickle of blood ran from the side of her mouth. Her breasts rose and fell beneath the thin material of her shirt and a vivid recollection of their full softness came uncomfortably to Lee.

Lee stepped back and passed a hand down his nail-scored face. He wiped away the blood. "You just missed my eyes," he accused.

"I wish I had taken both of them out, bounty hunter!" she snapped.

Lee couldn't help but grin at her female feistiness. "You and your baby brother just can't stand being left out of the act, can you?"

She smiled infuriatingly. "You didn't get Chad after all, did you, manhunter?"

He walked to her mare and led it back to her. "I will," he said quietly.

"Not in New Mexico you won't," she corrected. "And you don't dare go into Mexico after him."

"Get up," he ordered.

She got slowly to her feet. He picked up her Colt and emptied it and then shoved it into her holster. The rifle saddle scabbard was empty. He looked at her. She nodded and smiled. "Chad has it," she said sweetly.

He leaned against the mare. "You knew he was around here all the time, didn't you?" he asked.

She shrugged. "Not really. It was Gil who figured there was water here south of the S.P. and he also figured that Chad would have made it *across* the S.P. before moonrise. He was right. We came south instead of following the line of the railroad. Gil scouted you, mister, and you didn't even know it! We knew you'd kill Chad if he made a break for it. Gil led his bay close to the station and figured he'd head for the water, and he was right again. I led you away from the chase. Neat, don't you think?"

"Very," he agreed. "You run in better luck than I do, ma'am."

"It isn't luck, mister," she corrected. "Just brains."

He grinned. "You have great modesty as well as beauty," he said. "Now get up on that horse and don't try any tricks, Miss Luscombe, because you have worn my patience very thin. Now you and I are going to trail after Chad Mercer."

She stared at him. "You haven't a chance!" she cried.

He gave her a boot up into her saddle and looked up at

57

her with his scored face. "You really didn't think I was going to quit, did you?" he asked quietly. She drew back her head a little. He looked almost like a hunting wolf as he stood there with the moonlight glittering on his cold eyes. He turned without another word and mounted his dun.

There was a faint flush of cold gray dawn light in the eastern sky and a cutting wind swept down from the Florida Mountains driving fine grit across the barren flats. Lee Kershaw caught the odor of strong and pungent coffee on the dawn wind. A wraith of grayish smoke arose from an arroyo ahead of Lee and the woman. The faint sound of voices came on the wind. A horse whinnied and was immediately echoed by Leila's mare. A man thrust up his head from the arroyo. "Kershaw!" yelled Bert Dixon. "What happened to you?"

Lee reined in at the lip of the arroyo. Possemen stood sipping coffee about a dying fire. Their eyes flicked past Lee to his prisoner. Even with her swollen face and disheveled hair she was still a looker. Lee dismounted and held out a hand to her, but she ignored the hand and dismounted unassisted.

Gil Luscombe sat apart from the possemen with his eyes on Lee and Leila and as he saw Lee look at him he turned his head aside to hide a quick grin.

A round-faced older man eyed Lee. "That's Kershaw?" he asked. "Then, who the hell was that I talked to an hour ago?"

"Jesus Christ, Harry!" snapped Dixon. "That must have been Mercer you saw and talked to. Didn't you remember the description I gave you?"

"Harry can't hardly read, let alone remember anything like that! Godalmighty! Five thousand dollars right in his hands and he lets Mercer tell him he's Kershaw."

"How the hell was I to know?" exploded Harry.

Lee took his tin cup and filled it from the coffeepot. "You're sure it was him that got past you?" he asked Harry.

"It was him all right," said Dixon. "Some of us had

58

come south from the railway line after you left us. We figured you must know something. Harry wasn't with us when we talked to you along the S.P. line. He was riding west and then south when this hombre comes riding out of the brush hell for leather. He had the brass to stop and borrow some tobacco from Harry and then tells him to head east because *I* wanted to see him."

Lee looked at Harry. "What did he look like?"

"About your build, maybe a little taller but not as heavy as you. Light gray eyes. Blond hair and mustache. Riding a light bay."

"That was him all right," Lee said.

"How'd you miss him?" asked Dixon with a faintly malicious tone to his voice.

Lee glanced at Gil and then at Leila. "Bright boy there and his sister did the trick. Mercer was holed up in the old swing station just like I had figured he'd be. He was going to make his break for the border with his two horses. I killed one horse and the other stampeded. I had Mercer cold in that station when the kid and his smart sister butted in."

"Go on," urged Dixon. "The kid wouldn't talk. We found him on foot. He was carrying a rifle and leading a bare-backed claybank. It looked suspicious, so we picked him up."

Lee nodded. "That was Mercer's second horse. The kid turned loose his own horse and figured it would head for the water at the swing station and he was right. I could have nailed Mercer but the kid, or his sister, but most likely him, opened fire on me, chasing me into cover long enough for Mercer to make his break. He was smart enough to head west instead of south."

"And met good old Harry," growled one of the possemen.

"How'd I know who he was?" demanded Harry.

"He could have said he was Jesus Christ and you would have believed him!" snapped the posseman named Joe. "You just blew five thousand dollars, that's all!"

"Well, dammit, he showed me his star, didn't he?" demanded Harry.

One of the men spat to one side. "Likely he got the gawddamned star out'n a box of stale candy hawked at a burlecue show," he said disgustedly.

"Have you got anyone working west of here, Bert?" asked Lee.

"Who knows?" said Dixon. He threw up his arms. "My job was to patrol along the S.P. I'm not even sure there's *anyone* southwest of here." He looked toward the southwest. "You've got the Cedar Mountains west and southwest of here. Once he slips into them, you'll never find him."

Lee nodded thoughtfully. He looked sideways at the two Luscombes. "You picking up runaway kiddies to send home to their mommies and daddies?" he asked.

Bert shrugged. "I don't even know who they are," he replied. "The kid won't talk."

Lee stood up and tossed his coffee dregs to one side. If he told Dixon who they really were and Dixon took them back to Cibola, likely figuring there'd be some reward money paid for them, the kid at least would be in one helluva mess. Even Bennett Luscombe could hardly avoid having Gil charged with aiding and abetting the escape of Chad Mercer and, to make it worse, the kid had been deputized as well. The kid could always cover up for Leila, and Lee himself wouldn't say anything against her.

"Who are they?" asked Dixon. "What do you want me to do with them?"

Lee looked at Gil. "I don't know who they are," he lied. "All I know is they gave Mercer a chance to escape. Take 'em back with you and lock them up if you like, or let them go. It doesn't matter to me. Just keep those kiddies out of my hair."

Joe eyed Leila appreciatively. "Some kid," he said.

Gil slowly stood up. "Watch it, mister!" he warned.

Joe spat to one side. "What'll you do?" he asked.

Gil moved a little closer to him. Joe thoughtfully eyed the broad shoulders, the muscular frame, the big closed fists, and the pugnacious look on the kid's face. "Sorry, kid," he murmured. "No offense."

Lee mounted the dun. He touched it with his heels and rode along the arroyo toward the road. The wind shifted toward him just as one of the men spoke. "How the hell did Kershaw, *Lee* Kershaw, ever let Chad Mercer get away from that stage station?" he asked.

"He's just getting old, is all," said Gil Luscombe in a loud voice.

Lee turned in the saddle and rested a hand on his cantle pack to look back toward the group about the dying fire. The only persons to meet his look were the two Luscombes. Lee turned and rode out of the draw onto the road. Lee suddenly remembered another boy-man, or man-boy, years past who had defied Lee at times, and had fist-fought with Lee but had never beaten him, but who also had never been afraid of Lee, as a wiser person might have been when Lee's fighting blood was up. That man-boy had at last grown into a man. That same man had slipped through a net rigged for his capture, and by rights it should have caught him, but now he was in the open again and likely heading for the Cedar Mountains to find a hidden passage across the border into Chihuahua.

The sun climbed up and warmed Lee's back as he headed across the mesquite-studded sand flats toward the Cedars. He worked out a local map in his head as he rode along. The Cedars were part of the great Continental Divide running at an angle northwest-southeast from the Panhandle of Grant County slantways across the line dividing Grant and Luna counties, while the southwestern part of the Cedars reached into L-shaped Hidalgo County on the foot of the L. The Cedars also touched and crossed over another borderline—the one between New Mexico Territory and the Mexican State of Chihuahua. It was a barren country of broken mountains and dry desert, hardly inhabited by Mexicans and it was an isolated passageway between the adjacent corners of Arizona and New Mexico Territories into the Mexican state of Chihuahua. It was also a haunt of those tigers in human form—the predatory Chiricahua Apaches and their bloodthirsty kin, the deadly Yaquis of Sonora and Chihuahua.

Bert Dixon waited until Lee Kershaw was gone. He looked at his men. "The rest of you boys start south," he said casually.

"We won't catch Mercer now," said Joe.

"Get going!" said Dixon. "Mercer might double back. If the Rurales are patrolling the border, he might not be able to get across."

Dixon lighted a cigar as the possemen left the arroyo and turned south on the road. "What's so odd about you two?" he asked out of the side of his mouth as he lighted up.

"What do you mean?" asked Leila.

"I mean, what's your game?" asked the deputy.

"You're Lee Kershaw's amigo, not ours," said Gil shortly.

Dixon shrugged. "He's no great friend of mine." He kicked sand over the dying fire. "That damned fool Harry cost me and the boys five thousand bucks."

Gil casually eyed the deputy. "You want to sell your saddle and rifle?" he asked offhandedly.

"I'll need a saddle to get back to town," said Dixon.

Leila dusted off her riding skirt as she stood up. "There's one on a dead horse back at the stage station. It's a good one. A Frazier." She tucked back a loose wisp of hair and eyed Dixon.

"So there is!" cried Dixon. He looked at his saddle. "That's a good one too," he added.

"¿Cuanto?" snapped Gil quickly.

Dixon shrugged. He took out his cigar and eyed it as though he had never seen one before.

"A thousand bucks for the saddle and the rifle," offered Gil.

"And that also pays for you keeping your mouth shut," added Leila.

"You just talked me into it," said Dixon. He stripped the saddle from his horse and saddled up Gil's claybank. "Stay away from Columbus," he suggested.

Gil sat down and pulled off his left boot. He slid two fingers down inside a split seam and fished out some folded bills. He pulled on the boot and counted ten one-hundred-dollar bills. He handed the money to Dixon and shoved the rest of the money down inside a shirt pocket. Dixon slid the money into his coat pocket without taking his eyes from Gil's shirt pocket.

"That's the full price for the saddle and the gun and for keeping your mouth shut, isn't it, Mr. Dixon?" asked Leila from behind the deputy. Dixon nodded without looking back at her. "Then, get to hell out of the way," she suggested.

Dixon turned his head to look at her. His face paled. She held Gil's rifle in her hands and the muzzle was pointed toward Dixon. She half-cocked the heavy weapon. He looked into those green eyes and felt a little weak in the kidneys. "I'll give you back the money," he offered hastily.

Gil cinched tight the saddle and came up under the claybank's belly. He grinned at Dixon. "She means it," he said.

Dixon nodded as he stepped aside. She mounted her horse and slid the rifle into its scabbard. She and her brother rode toward the mouth of the arroyo.

"¡Vaya con Dios!" Dixon called out.

They waved their hands without turning.

Dixon cupped his hands about his mouth. "That's Apache country!" he yelled.

Gil waved a casual hand as they crossed the road and started across the mesquite flats.

A cold gust of wind swept down the arroyo, driving grit before it and stirring up the last of the smoke from the half-buried fire. Dixon shivered a little. He shook his head as he watched the two riders on the flats. "Vaya con Dios," he said soberly. This time he surely meant it.

NINE

THE LATE AFTERNOON slanted down on the western face of the Cedar Mountains. Heat waves shimmered upward from the naked slopes and from the wide and barren valley west of the mountains. Lee Kershaw shoved back his hat and let the hot, stinging sweat run down his scored face and into his ragged beard, where it brought out a persistent itching. He passed a dry tongue along cracked lips. A dust devil swirled up out of nowhere and raced across the flats only to vanish as quickly as it had appeared. Lee snapped his field glasses up to his eyes. There was nothing out on the flats that had caused the dust to rise—nothing but the wind itself.

The dun was wearing out. Now and then he stumbled a little as he crossed the baking sand flats. Lee had pushed him hard all that day. Something caught Lee's eyes as he glanced upward at the pitiless sky. It was a black, skyborne speck that lifted and fell a little in the wind currents like a dried leaf. Lee narrowed his burning eyes. "*¡Zopilote!*" he husked. The great Sonoran buzzard tilted up on one black, white-tipped wing and veered off on the hot wind. Something was holding his interest far out on those baking sand barrens—something dead or dying. Lee raised the field glasses but could not pick up anything through the shimmering heat veils that arose from the ground.

Lee touched the dun with his heels. "Just a little longer, amigo," he said.

The dun ran steadily but not easily. Now and then he tossed at the bit. His ears seemed to wilt now and then. His gait became a little unsteady. Lee loosed the bit and drew up his weight. In a little while the dun seemed to find a new reservoir of wind and endurance. The *zopilote* was now swinging in ever-narrower circles and lower and lower toward the ground. Then the buzzard banked and veered swiftly off between a pair of low, well-rounded hills and was gone from Lee's sight.

The sun seemed to be stuck on the western mountains. The dun outstretched his head as though to pull himself on by sheer willpower. His breathing was rasping and uneven. He was starting to blow.

The sun finally slid down behind the western range. Lee rounded the first of the low twin hills. Something dark lay heaped on the naked ground. The *zopilote* swung upward and away as he saw Lee approaching. Lee reined in and eased himself a little stiffly to the ground. His gait was a little awkward as he walked toward the fallen horse. He took out his tobacco canteen and shaped a quirly as he studied the fallen light bay. It had been saddle-stripped. It looked like the bay Mercer had ridden from the stage station, and the posseman named Harry had said Mercer had been riding a light bay.

Shadows were flowing down the long slopes like viscous lava, filling in the deep hollows and creeping out onto the flats, reaching out on either flank to touch other growing shadows preparatory to inking in the whole valley for the premoon darkness. The sun was now gone. A faint stirring of lethargic wind came with the disappearance of the sun. Lee lighted the cigarette while he looked south along the darkening valley. The border could not be more than six or seven miles away. Lee picked up the reins and looked at the dun. "The sonofabitch is walking now and carrying his saddle and rifle. Can you make still another try, amigo?" he asked. He mounted the dun and rode south. Mercer would be desperate for water and a horse. If he went west, he'd only be trending deeper into Hidalgo County. To reach Mexico he had to go due south. To get to the nearest waterhole he'd have to slant to the southwest.

Lee rode for half an hour and then dismounted to take the reins and lead the dun while he set off in a swinging mile-eating stride. He was *na-tse-kes* in his mind now. It was the Apache way; *na-tse-kes*—to think about one thing, and one thing only, to the absolute exclusion of everything else. That one thought was Chad Mercer. Somehow, in the absorbing metamorphosis of tracking down Chad Mercer, Lee had forgotten everything else—the Querencia in particular. What was important now was to win the game, one man against another, the hunter versus the hunted, with death for one or the other as the loser's penalty.

By the time the moon was beginning to feel its way down into the Playas Valley, Lee knew that Mexico, in a sense, was now *behind* him, due east, as well as at his left, to the south, while he was now trending southwest further into Hidalgo County, beyond which was the eastern border of Arizona Territory. There was a waterhole there in the barren nakedness of the hills; a shallow *tinaja* that was usually dry during the heat of the summer and the early fall.

Lee's thirst was a torturing thing as he led the dun into a shallow canyon and then picketed it. He poured the very last of his water into his dusty hat and let the dun drink it. When the dun was through drinking, Lee raised the empty hat and licked at the few remaining drops. He took his rifle and then catfooted out of the canyon and up a long boulder-strewn slope that crested abruptly in a broken rampart of serrated rock that looked like a sawblade against the sky. Lee reached the reverse crest and went to ground in a jumble of broken and shattered rock, feeling the trapped heat of it and waiting, almost expectantly, to hear the dry war rattles of a disturbed, thick-bodied diamondback rattler.

Lee peered down into the next canyon. Two hundred yards below his position the first of the moonlight was beginning to silver the shallow, sheeted water of a wide *tinaja,* which was sheltered within a pair of tall rock pinnacles beyond which was a steeply pitched slope of detritus that eventually met a vertical rock wall that rose sheer to a serrated escarpment. The water in the *tinaja* was likely to be gamey and thick with wrigglers, but a desperate man could survive on it.

Nothing moved within the canyon as the moonlight filled it. There was a dreamlike atmosphere about the canyon and there was no wind, not even a breath of moving air to ruffle the surface of the *tinaja* water. It looked like a sheet of burnished metal under the full light of the moon. Something clicked sharply on the far side of the canyon and the sound carried clearly to Lee. He studied the outer flanks of the rock pinnacles that semicircled the waterhole. A stone came bounding down the slope and clicked sharply as it rebounded from a boulder. The acoustics of the canyon carried every little sound clearly to Lee. Minutes dragged past. A shadow on the east side of the pinnacles suddenly fattened. A tall man stepped silently out into the bright moonlight. Lee raised his field glasses, focused them, and found himself looking at the bristle-bearded face of Chad Mercer.

Mercer knelt beside the *tinaja* and scooped up water to his mouth. Lee looked quickly away. The silvery drippings from Mercer's mouth and beard made Lee's throat constrict. When Lee looked down again, Mercer was filling one of his canteens. Lee rested his Winchester on a notched rock and raised the buckhorn rear sight for a two-hundred-yard downhill shot. There was no wind. It wasn't too difficult for a killing shot, but Lee did not want to kill him—not yet, at least. Lee would try for a flesh wound. He closed his eyes to rest them, but they burned as though they were on fire. He opened his eyes and studied Mercer, then took up the trigger slack, lowering the rifle a mite to compensate for the tendency to fire high when firing downhill. He sighted on Mercer's extended left arm and then slowly tightened his right hand about the small of the stock and began to squeeze the trigger as if he had a firm rubber ball enclosed within his big hand.

Mercer stood up and turned quickly just as Lee anticipated the crashing discharge of the .44/40 cartridge. Mercer snatched up his canteens and rifle and then moved so swiftly that Lee did not have time to sight on him again. Mercer darted around the eastern side of the pinnacles and was gone out of Lee's sight.

Lee cursed softly as he heard the faint sound of voices

from the broken slopes to his left. He edged forward and saw two familiar figures standing at the mouth of a deep draw. "Damn them to everlasting hell," he grated out. He looked quickly toward the *tinaja*. Mercer had not reappeared at the *tinaja,* nor was there any sign of him beyond the pinnacles.

Lee looked toward the two Luscombes. Gil was pointing down toward the waterhole. There was no sign of any horses. Likely they had not seen Mercer, but he had heard them and it had stampeded him. Lee looked again toward the pinnacles and a curious and uneasy feeling came over him. He could not explain it, but he knew somehow that something was wrong. He looked to his right and down along the canyon floor. Mercer had quickly looked that way before he had vanished behind the pinnacles. Lee raised his field glasses and promptly forgot all about Chad Mercer. An icy fist seemed to grip his lower guts and pressure them, twisting them and turning them and always increasing the pressure. A man was standing at the wide western mouth of the canyon looking toward the *tinaja.* There was no question about his race or tribe! He wore no hat and his thick mane of black hair was bound back from his broad forehead by a dingy band of white cloth. Even as Lee stared at him he vanished with an utterly silent, catlike stride into the litter of broken rock just beyond the mouth of the canyon.

Lee vaulted over the rock ledge in front of him and ran anglewise down the treacherous slope toward the two Luscombes. Gil turned quickly, saw Lee and then raised his rifle. Lee waved his free hand and stabbed a pointing finger back behind himself down toward the canyon mouth. He then waved to them to get back into the draw. They did not move. Lee plunged through a thicket of cruel crucifixion thorns and felt them tearing viciously at his thigh-length moccasins.

"Stay where you are, Kershaw!" warned Gil.

Lee landed light-footed within twenty feet of them. "For God's sake!" he warned. "Get back! Get back out of sight!"

"What the hell game are you pulling?" demanded the kid.

Lee leaned forward. "Apaches, mister!" he snarled. "Now get to hell out of sight! *I* am! If they see you and hear that big mouth of yours, I aim to be a half a mile from here and moving faster every minute!"

Gil grinned. "Look at him, sis!" he jeered. "He's *afraid!* The big, bad manhunter is afraid of a few stinking Apache bucks!"

"So am I," said Leila soberly.

Lee brushed past the two of them. "Where are your horses?" he demanded.

"Half a mile on the other side of the ridge," replied Leila.

"He's pulling some kind of a game, sis," warned Gil.

Lee whirled. He hit the kid with a driving left hook that knocked him ass-flat on the hard ground. He pointed, without speaking, toward the west as the kid, with fire in his eyes, began to get to his feet. The lone Apache had reappeared, moving across the rough ground as effortlessly as though he were suspended above it. He stopped near the *tinaja.* The quavering cry of a coyote arose from his mouth and it was so natural-sounding that one might really believe that he was Brother Coyote in human form.

"Dear God," said Leila faintly. She stepped behind a boulder.

The coyote cry echoed through the canyon and died away. Seconds later the cry echoed from further down the canyon, and then from up the canyon beyond where Lee and the two Luscombes stood. The lone Apache near the *tinaja* turned and looked up the moonlighted slopes toward where Lee Kershaw stood half in and half out of the faint shadow of a boulder. "Don't move a muscle," warned Lee out of the side of his mouth. It seemed to Lee that the buck was staring right at him. Lee did not move; he almost stopped breathing; he did not blink an eye. For a long, long moment the buck looked directly at Lee and then he turned toward the *tinaja.* Lee dropped to the ground and looked sideways at the kid, who lay bellyflat just beyond him. "Some game," breathed Lee. "Stand up, stand up for Jesus, little man, and you'll have the pack of them hot on your heels within seconds."

"I only saw one," said the kid.

"You heard two more," said Lee. Lee peered around the boulder. "Keep your head down," he warned over his shoulder. "Take a quick look, sonny."

A file of bucks had appeared at the mouth of the canyon. They led their soft-footed horses up the canyon. Now and then one of the Apaches would look up at the moonlighted heights and the moon would strike his broad, dark-skinned face marked ghostlike with a band of white bottom clay across the nose and cheekbones.

The Apaches did not all drink at once. Some of them stood watch while the others drank. No sound carried to the three white people on the northern slopes of the canyon. There was an eerie, haunting quality about the scene.

"Where is Chad?" whispered Leila.

Lee looked back at her. "Somewhere beyond those rock pinnacles," he replied.

"Are you sure?" she asked.

Lee nodded. "Positive!"

"Will they find him?"

"I don't know how they can miss," he said quietly. He wormed his way into the shadows of two boulders and raised his field glasses, turning them away from the direct light of the moon to keep the moonlight from reflecting from the lenses. He focused them on the pinnacles. Something moved ever so slightly atop the easternmost pinnacle. Chad Mercer lay there, almost as though blended into the rocks themselves. He was not fifty feet away from the closest Apache. "He's there," whispered Lee. "Atop the easternmost pinnacle."

The Apaches were in no hurry. After the horses had been watered the bucks squatted beside the waterhole, although some of them were always on guard. "Don't move and don't talk," whispered Lee. He grinned, despite his own fear. They were really listening to him now.

"They might stay there all night," blurted out Gil.

"Shut up!" hissed Lee. He shook his head. "They never camp near water," he added. "That's a white man's fool stunt."

Lee lowered the glasses. Had Mercer seen Lee when Lee had run across to the draw? Even as the thought went through his mind there was a quick movement atop the pinnacle. Lee raised his glasses. Something down there reflected moonlight like a drop of mercury. Mercer had raised his own field glasses and was looking directly up toward the draw. Lee was sure now that Mercer had seen the three of them there before they had taken cover.

The moonlight drifted slowly from the sloped area behind the rock pinnacles to leave the broken slopes dark in the shadow of the southern wall of the canyon. There was the faintest of movements atop the easternmost pinnacle. Lee focused his glasses on it. "He's making his move," whispered Lee. It took guts to move about with those human bloodhounds within spitting distance, but now Mercer must know that he was being watched by Lee from the draw. He would risk a retreat, using the Apaches to cover him, for he knew well enough that Lee could not risk pursuing him.

Once Lee saw, or *thought* he saw, Mercer spread-eagled against the dark southern wall of the canyon. All one of the Apaches had to do was to glance casually in that direction. If a stone dropped to the rocky slopes below, the sound would carry clearly to the Apaches. Lee focused the glasses on the southern rim of the canyon and thought he saw Mercer roll quickly over the lip of it and then vanish from sight. In a little while he stood up, plainly revealed in the moonlight but standing back far enough from the rim so that he could not be seen by the Apaches down at the *tinaja*. Mercer was looking directly toward where Lee and the two Luscombes were hidden. Chad casually waved a hand and then he lifted his rifle. He aimed and fired and the crashing discharge echoed and reechoed between the canyon walls. The slug keened off rock not a foot from Lee's head and tiny lead shards stung his face. He involuntarily jerked away and got up on one knee in full sight of the Apaches. As the shot echo died away Lee was almost positive he could hear faint laughter coming from the southern heights of the canyon, but there was no one standing there.

Four bucks ran across the canyon floor toward the slopes beneath the draw. Three other bucks flung themselves on their horses and rode toward the western mouth of it. Lee snatched up his rifle. He looked sideways at Leila. "They've seen me. They might not have seen you two. Can you run in that rig?" She nodded. "Then, run like you've never run before!" he snapped. He shoved her up the draw. Gil gripped Lee's left arm. "We can hold them off here," he suggested. Lee shook his head. "They're circling around on both flanks to get behind us. You *might* make it to your horses." Gil wasted no time in running up the draw after his sister.

Lee fired twice down the slopes without taking aim to slow down the bucks on foot. He plowed up the draw, slipping and sliding on the loose rock. Leila had reached the top where the draw notched the rim. She stopped and looked back with fear etched on her face. "Run, damn you, run!" yelled Lee hoarsely. She wasted no time. Gil disappeared after her.

Lee reached the top. He whirled and fired twice down the trough of the draw and then he plunged down the reverse slope in great, leaping bounds, hurdling rocks with feet to spare, crashing through the clinging catclaw and crucifixion brush that ripped into his clothing and flesh like steel-tipped darts. He braked his descent on a talus slope, raising a bitter cloud of dust behind him. He shot a glance to the right. Leila was legging it through a tangle of brush into the shelter of some scrub trees and Gil was racing after her. Even as Lee looked at them they vanished from his sight seconds before the four Apaches crested the rim above the three fugitives.

Lee ran north toward the shallow canyon where he had left the dun. He glanced to his left. Mounted bucks were lashing their swift ponies along the foot of the ridge. He looked to the right. More mounted bucks were passing the thick patch of brush and scrub trees into which Leila and Gil had disappeared. They had but one quarry now—Lee

Kershaw. A wild and weird crying came from the pursuing bucks who were leaping down the slope from the rim. The devils could outrun a horse on such slopes.

Lee hurdled a ledge and then turned. He fired two times at the bucks to his right and then two times at the bucks to his left and saw a horse go down thrashing atop its rider. He snapped a shot up the slopes and then plunged on to the north with his breathing coming out of his throat like flares of fire from a heated brass tube. He reached the dun, ripped loose the picket pin, and then mounted. He turned in the saddle and fired until he ran dry the rifle magazine with the booming echoes tumbling one over the other in the narrow canyon. The powder-smoke swirled up behind Lee as he rode up the canyon, smashing the rifle butt against the dusty flanks of the dun.

By the sheer grace of God he saw a narrow cleft of a canyon mouth off to his left and he turned into it, hoping by all that was holy that it was not a waterless box canyon. He let the reins rest on the neck of the dun and then fed fresh cartridges into the empty maw of the Winchester magazine.

By the time the moon was gone, his horse was almost done in. Lee dismounted and looked back down the canyon. It was dark in shadow, but there was no sight or sound of pursuit. The cold feeling stole through him that they might have seen Gil and Leila and gone back after them. He wiped the sweat from his face and rested his throbbing head against the sweat-soaked saddle. For a few moments he stood there feeling the erratic thudding of his heart against his ribs and then he forced himself to take the reins and to lead the dun as Lee struck out at full stride, driving himself on and on with his last reserves of strength while the hot, stinging sweat ran down his dirty, bearded face and his body to raise anew the stale stink of his clothing while the salt of it stung the scratches on his face and the thorn rips on his body.

Before he stopped to rest in the thick darkness, he had worked far to the west and then to the south, circling wide around that Apache-haunted canyon that held the water-hole. That waterhole might be the only one for many square miles. Now and again during his flight he had stopped to listen for pursuit, but all he had ever heard had been his own labored breathing and that of the dun, except for now and then the murmurings of the dry night wind.

TEN

THE EARLY MORNING SUN was already striking at man and horse with deadly heat when Lee turned loose the dun, slapping him on a dusty flank as he trotted past down the long mesquite-studded slope on the south side of the low mountain. To Lee's left as he slogged on after the dun were further water rutted slopes that gradually reached the fan-shaped *bajada arenosa* that spread out across the barren flats.

The dun was moving a little faster now. Lee wiped the sweat from his face and hurried on after the horse. The dun whinnied softly. Lee narrowed his eyes. There was a rock outcropping further down the slope and it seemed to Lee that there was a faint tinge of blessed green showing against the dominant reddish yellow of the slope. He began to run. The dun disappeared around the rock formation. Lee plunged on, passing a dirty hand across his swollen, cracked lips. He rounded the rock formation and saw the dun standing spraddle-legged with his head low, drinking steadily from a shallow pothole.

Lee hit the warm rock surface bellyflat to lie beside the dun. He pushed back the thin covering of greenish matter and tasted the water. It was gamey and he could see wrigglers writhing about on the bottom, but if the dun would drink it, it must be potable. Lee drank only a little of it. The taste was tolerable. He sat up and untied his neck scarf. He rinsed out the scarf in the shallow water and then tied it about his big tin cup. He submerged his smaller canteen in the water and let it fill, then slowly poured the water through the scarf into the tin cup. When the cup had been filled, he removed the scarf and wiped it fairly clean, then carefully poured the strained water into his larger canteen.

The dun drank a little more and then began to crop at the scant fringe of greenery near the waterhole. Lee filled the smaller canteen and strained the water through the scarf. He capped the large canteen. The dun suddenly raised his head and looked toward the eastern flank of the mountain slope. Lee placed a hand on his Winchester. A thread of dust rose from behind a gaunt rock outcropping. Lee led the dun into cover and picketed him. Quickly Lee filled the small canteen with the gamey water and then he himself went to cover.

The dust increased and drifted lazily off on the fitful wind. Lee sucked at his neck scarf to get the moisture out of it. The sun burned through the thinness of his shirt.

A man leading a horse appeared at the bottom of the outcropping and looked out across the far-stretching heat-shimmering flats to the south. Lee raised his field glasses and focused them on the man. "I'll be dipped in fresh manure," he muttered. The good lenses had caught the dusty, sunburned face of young Gil Luscombe. As Lee watched the kid he saw Leila appear behind him. She was leading a limping roan horse. The two Luscombes stood there looking uncertainly about them and then across that heat-shimmering suburb of hell toward Mexico. Gil looked sideways at his sister and pointed north. Leila shook her head. She stepped back into the hot shade of the ledge and passed a slim hand across her burning eyes. She was suffering damnably, but it was quite evident that she would not go back. "True love," murmured Lee. He shook his head.

Gil walked partway down the slope and then paused, turning to look directly toward Lee. Lee lay still. The kid was worried. He looked back at his sister. The bullheaded punk might be beginning to feel the heavy responsibility he had so casually assumed back in the Querencia when the two of them had decided to trail Lee Kershaw to keep him from capturing Chad Mercer.

Lee studied them through the glasses. They'd have to go back. The problem was that there wasn't any water within perhaps forty miles, with the exception of the Apache-haunted *tinaja* and the pothole where Lee lay hidden. Lee studied the woman. She had guts, he had to admit to himself. He got slowly to his feet, waved his hat, and yelled at the two Luscombes. His hoarse voice carried clearly along the hot slopes. The two of them faded quickly behind the rock ledge.

Lee walked out into the open, risking a rifle bullet. "It's Lee Kershaw!" he yelled. "There's some water here!"

Gil stuck out his head and looked up at Lee. Lee held up his big canteen and shook it. That was enough for the two of them. They came along the slope with the worn-out horses behind them. When they reached the waterhole, Lee had filled his big cup with strained water. He did not look back at them. "Coyote tea," he said over his shoulder. "There might be enough left for you to fill yourselves, your canteens, and that roan mare."

They did not move. Lee looked up at them. "Come on," he invited. "I'm straining this for myself. No room service here, friends."

They squatted beside the shallow rock pan as Lee stood up. Leila stripped the scarf from about her neck. Her sunburned nose wrinkled as she looked at the unappetizing, smelly water. Gil floated back the green scum and the pinkish floating bladders. He sipped at the water. "Coyote tea," he agreed. "If you hold your nose, sis, it ain't too bad." He grinned up at Lee. "Beats me why an animal would want to pee in his only water supply," he said.

Lee shrugged. "Perhaps to show his true feelings toward us humans," he suggested.

"That's a big thought," said Gil.

"I have a big mind," countered Lee. He drained the cup and handed it to Leila. He walked back into the hot shade and placed his back against warm rock as he sat

76

down with his long legs stretched out in front of him. He began to shape a cigarette as he watched the two of them patiently straining water into the first of their canteens.

Leila brushed back a strand of hair and looked sideways at Lee with those great green eyes of hers. "Thanks," she said.

"Por nada," replied Lee. He lighted his cigarette.

"I also meant that for what you did for us back there," she added.

"Por nada," repeated Lee. "Tobacco, kid?" he asked.

Gil nodded. He deftly caught the little tobacco canteen and the packet of sweat-damp cigarette papers. "It took guts to do what you did back there, Kershaw," he said. "You could have gotten away by yourself without warning us."

Lee waved a hand. "We could have sat them out if it hadn't been for your hero Chad Mercer," he said dryly.

Leila looked quickly at him. "Why do you say that?" she asked.

Lee shrugged. "That shot he fired at me might have been to kill me, but I doubt it. He fired to flush me out so that those Chiricahuas could see me. He did a beautiful job."

She narrowed her lovely green eyes. "Are you trying to tell me that Chad actually *exposed* you to the Apaches?"

"I'm not *trying* to tell you. I *am* telling you," he replied.

"I don't believe it!" she cried.

Lee blew a smoke ring and poked a dirty finger into it. "That was Chad Mercer up on that southern rim," he explained. "He must have seen me from the top of those pinnacles when I ran to warn you two. When he got back up on that rim, he must have figured the odds. He was afoot. His horse had dropped dead under him back in the Playas Valley. If he was seen by the Apaches while he was up on that rim, they would have circled around behind him and got him before he could have gotten into the clear. He also figured something else—I was closer on his trail than he realized. So he exposed me by firing at me. The Apaches went after us. He beat it to hell to the

77

south. By God's luck we made it away from there. You can figure right now you're living on borrowed time, ma'am."

She sipped a little of the gamey water. She wrinkled her sunburned nose. "You tell a good story, Mr. Kershaw," he said. "But I still don't believe it." She looked at Gil as though for verification.

Gil lighted a cigarette and flipped away the match. "Kershaw is right, sis," he said quietly.

"Chad wouldn't do a thing like that!" she cried. She looked quickly at Lee. "He used *you* as a decoy, not *us*!"

Gil shook his head. "I think he knew why Kershaw left his cover to come to us. He knows Lee well enough to know that Lee would never have exposed himself like that if he had been alone. Furthermore, sis, if Chad saw Lee, *he must have seen us as well*." The kid took the cigarette from his mouth and looked at it almost as though he had never seen one like it before. "All Chad was doing was thinking of himself. The three of us might have been killed or caught back there. They would have killed me and Lee right off, sis." He looked sideways at his sister. "There must have been a dozen of them there. You know what would have happened to you? You might have lived long enough to have been used by every one of them. If you weren't dead or dying after that, they would have killed you or left you to die alone."

Lee eyed Leila. "The kid is right," he agreed.

"You'd say that anyway!" she snapped.

"He's still right," said Gil.

"Are you turning against me, too?" she demanded.

He stood up and handed her the tin cup. "Fill that big canteen," he ordered. "No one is turning against you, sis. Just face the truth! You seem to be able to do that most of the time—except when it comes to Chad Mercer." He walked over to the roan mare and the claybank.

She looked at Lee, but Lee looked away from her. She wasn't too bright in some ways, he thought. But then she was a young woman in love. That answered the whole problem and logic be damned.

Gil led the horses to the water as Leila finished filling

the big canteen. Gil passed a hand down the dun's neck. "All right to water him?" he asked.

Lee nodded. "But slow, boy. Slow——"

"I know horses!" rapped out Gil. "And don't call me 'boy'!"

Lee grinned. He stood up and stretched his long legs. "How'd you happen to come this way?" he asked.

"Dumb luck," replied Gil. "We just let the horses have their heads."

Lee nodded. *"That,* at least, was smart," he said.

Leila stoppered a canteen. "Was he here?" she asked without looking at Lee.

Lee led the dun away from the water and hooked his filled canteens to the saddle. "He was," he replied.

"How do you know?" demanded Gil.

"Intuition," replied Lee.

"You're not that smart," jeered Gil.

Lee walked over to where he had been lying watching the two Luscombes when they had first appeared. He reached down behind a boulder and lifted a dusty saddle. He threw it down in front of Gil. "His," he said laconically. "Beats the hell out of me why he carried it this far."

"Where'd he go?" asked Gil as he looked about.

Lee jerked a thumb to point south down the dusty slopes.

"What's that way beside the damned desert?" asked the kid.

"Mexico," replied Lee as he took his moccasins from his saddle. He sat down on a flat rock and pulled off his boots. He replaced the boots with the moccasins.

Gil eyed the moccasins. "You a breed?" he asked carelessly.

Lee looked up. "That ain't exactly a polite question to ask a man," he said.

"Well?" asked Gil.

Lee shook his head. "These are *n'deh b'keh,*" he explained. "Best footgear in the world for this kind of country."

"Sneaky, too, ain't they?" asked the kid.

Lee shrugged. "Maybe you're getting the idea, kid."

"Where'd you get 'em?" persisted Gil. "Off a corpse?"

Lee half grinned. "That's taboo, kid. Best way to get a good pair like these is to give a horse or a mule to the father of an Apache virgin and have her make them for you from the skin of a deer you killed yourself and skinned with the proper ritual."

Gil glanced at his sister. Leila was standing fifty feet away looking out across the heat-blasted plains to the south. Gil grinned a little evilly. "What'd you give the virgin?" he asked in a low voice. "Or maybe what I mean is, what'd you take *away* from her?"

Lee folded the top of one moccasin down about his left knee and bound it there with a thong. "Not an *Apache* virgin, kid," he replied. "You might chase a Navajo virgin and pay off the old man after you caught her, but don't try that little game amongst the Apaches."

"Hell! I thought they were all the same!"

Lee fastened the second moccasin about his right knee. "Try it and find out," he suggested.

"I ain't *that* stupid!" The kid studied Lee. "You know a lot about Apaches, don't you?"

Lee shrugged. "It's kept me alive in their country," he replied. He took out his knife and slit the lining of one of his boots.

"You actually going into Mexico?" asked Gil.

Lee looked up. "He's there, isn't he?" he said.

"They'll give you the *ley del fuego* if they catch you," warned the kid.

Lee unpinned his deputy star and pinned it inside the lining of the boot. He slit the lining of the other boot and placed the warrant within it. He took needle and thread from a shirt pocket and deftly stitched the boot linings back into place.

"You sew like a little old lady," commented Gil.

"I was nigh seven years old before my mother would admit that I was a boy," said Lee dryly. He tied his boots together and fastened them to his saddle. "She had always wanted a girl," he added.

Gil grinned. "I believe it," he said.

Lee glanced sideways at him. "Fact," he said.

Lee dropped flat beside the pool and drank a little of the water. Gil looked to the south. "Welcome to romantic Mexico," he murmured. "Laughing señoritas with flashing eyes; gay guitar music played by handsome caballeros; exotic foods and liquors that inspire."

Lee stood up and wiped his mouth with the back of a hand. "Don't forget the welcoming committee, kid—the Rurales, the Federales, the Apaches, and the Yaquis."

"You really going across the border?" asked Gil.

"Watch me," said Lee. He leaned back against his saddle shaping a cigarette. "You've got enough water to get back if you ration it. How are you fixed for rations?"

"Nada," replied Gil.

Lee lighted his cigarette and then began to unstrap a saddlebag.

"Forget it," said Leila from behind Lee.

Lee turned and looked at her. He nodded. He re-strapped the saddlebag. "Maybe you should lose a little weight at that," he said as he eyed her slightly rounded belly.

She flushed a little as she walked to her roan.

"You know where the next waterhole south is?" asked the kid.

Lee nodded. "I think I can find it, but you can't be sure there'll be water there at this time of the year." He picked up the reins and led the dun down the slope. "I'll likely see you in Cibola in a couple of weeks," he added. The shimmering heat waves struck up under his hat brim as they rose from the baking ground. He could feel the heat of the desert floor rising even through the thick soles of his desert moccasins. At the bottom of the slope, as he figured it, he'd be in Mexico, State of Chihuahua. He turned to look back as he reached the level ground at the bottom of the slope. "Madre de Dios!" he cried out.

The two of them were coming down the slope behind him. He waited for them. They halted twenty feet from him. "Go on back," said Lee. Gil shook his head. He looked sideways at Leila as though to indicate to Lee that it was she who wanted to go on, therefore he *had* to go with her.

Lee shoved back his hat and the collected sweat ran stinging down his face into his beard. He jerked his head backwards. "You know what that is out there?" he asked. "I'll tell you! It's the Llanos de Carretas, cursed by the sun, as waterless as the moon, and haunted by the Apaches and the Yaquis. The Mexicans say that God finished creating the world and had some useless muck left over which he had to get rid of, so he dumped it out here in western Chihuahua and eastern Sonora, figuring no one would ever live here. He was right about that."

They did not move or speak.

"Go on back," Lee insisted. He placed his hand on the butt of his Colt.

They stood there looking at him.

Lee wiped the sweat from his face. "God's Blood!" he said in Spanish. "I'm dealing with fools or madmen. I will not take you with me across these accursed plains!"

"You don't have to," she said. "Is Chad south of us?"

"I wouldn't be here if I didn't think so," he replied.

"You can't stop us from following you," said Gil.

He looked at those two stubborn, taut faces and knew well enough they meant what they had said. Without a further word he turned and picked up the dun's reins. He looped them over his left arm and felt within his shirt for his plug of Wedding Cake as he walked on. He cut a big chew and stuffed it into his mouth to keep the moisture within it. He worked loose the "sauce" of the tobacco chew. As he swung along in a seemingly tireless stride across those flat and baking plains, every now and then he'd turn his head a little to one side or the other to spit. Behind him, on either side of the faint tracks he and the dun left there were brown stains of the tobacco juice and by the time the two people who were following him reached the juice, the burning sun had driven the moisture of the juice down into the thirsty caliche, leaving only the stain of it to be seen.

One foot in front of the other, hour after hour, without looking up except at long intervals for telltale signs of rising dust other than that of the ubiquitous dust devils that constantly swirled across the sun-baked, heat-shimmering flats that were as naked of growth as a billiard ball. In the late afternoon a mirage arose in the far southern reaches of the Llanos de Carretas. It looked like a wide lake of clear, shimmering blue water, but in reality it was the sun's rays reflecting from an ancient salt lake, one of the Devil's trick props to delude travelers on that highway of hell.

By the time the sun had slanted down over the barren western mountains, Lee's water was all gone. Darkness fled swiftly across the llano. Lee's moccasined feet struck faint ruts. He walked across the ancient road, leading the head-hanging, stumbling dun. Suddenly the dun raised his head. He nickered plaintively. Lee plodded up a long slope. The darkness of a shallow canyon showed at his feet. He turned and plodded down the slope until his feet struck the ruts. He followed the ruts in a semicircle until they led him to the dark mouth of the canyon. The dun nickered again. Lee halted and nose-clamped the horse. Lee stood there with his head raised a little, listening to the faint sounds of the night.

Lee went on. The canyon widened on either hand. A dry wind moaned fitfully down the canyon. The dun nickered sharply. Lee turned to softly curse the horse and as he turned back again to lead the way he rammed his bearded face hard against a wall. He passed questioning hands down the surface to distinguish if it was formed of adobe bricks or if it was a natural formation. His broken fingernails traced the lines of a course of wide bricks. He sidled along the wall until he reached the corner and the breeze dried the sweat on his face. He strained his eyes through the velvety darkness and began to pick out rectangular shapes set in a more or less regular pattern. He touched his cracked lips with trembling fingers. He turned and slapped the dun on the dusty rump and jerked his rifle from its scabbard as the dun trotted past.

Lee walked softly through the darkness, guided only by the soft hoofbeats of the dun. The dun veered to the right and up a gentle slope. Lee halted. The sound of the hoofbeats came to him on the wind. Lee began to hurry despite his innate caution in such hostile country. "Damn you!" he cursed himself. He walked forward, swinging his shaggy head from side to side. "Where are you?" he asked in a cracked voice. The dun nickered from the darkness. Lee made him out. He was standing with hanging head. Oh God, thought Lee—*there's no water!* A moment later he was splashing knee-deep in an unseen pool of water.

ELEVEN

LEE RAISED HIS dripping head from the pool of water. There was a faint trace of the rising moon far to the east across miles and miles of windy darkness. Lee sat up and wiped his mouth with the back of a hand and then squeezed out the water from his ragged beard. He looked back over his shoulder and as he did so he caught the faintest spark of light far to the south through the shallow gap of the canyon. It was so instantaneous and gone so swiftly that he wasn't even sure he had seen it at all. He got to his feet and led the dun away from the water to keep it from foundering itself. He picketed the dun on a scant patch of grazing and then removed saddle and saddle blanket. He rubbed down the dun and fed him the last of the sugar.

As the moonlight grew, Lee eye-scouted the area. He was in a *poblado* that looked like it had been abandoned for decades, but Lee knew better. The ruins stretched on each side of a long and narrow street that was actually part of the road that drifted south on the Llanos de Carretas to the water that was spring-fed in the canyon; and then the road continued on, as straight as a string across the southern Llanos for long and empty miles.

Lee shaped and lighted a cigarette as he walked slowly down the street, skirting the shattered wreckage of a carreta that lay atop one crumpled wheel and with its shafts pointing up toward the night sky like the antennae of some strange insect. A church stood at the southern end of the *poblado* with a weed-grown Campo Santo beside it. The dry night wind whispered through the openings in the bell tower. Not a sign of life showed anywhere in the area.

Lee walked back up the street toward the springs. The moonlight was beginning to flood out on the Llanos de Carreta and the silvery light showed that the plains were as empty of life as the moon itself. Now and then Lee would quickly turn his head to look past the buildings with their empty windows looking back at him like the eye sockets of a skull. There was never anything there, but there was always the feeling that something *had* been there, just out of eyeshot as Lee turned.

Lee risked a small fire of dried wood in a crumbling casa to heat his beans and his coffee and as soon as they were ready, he put out the fire and kicked dirt over it to kill the smoldering. He squatted beside the fireplace on the eroded packed-earth flooring and ate while he looked through the gaping openings in the north and east walls of the casa. Nothing moved out there except the night wind. He set aside half his beans for a cold breakfast and then lighted a cigarette as he walked to the moonlighted pool. The pool was large, larger than he had remembered it to be, and was fed from an underground spring that emerged from the sloping canyon wall that ranked itself behind the western side of the *poblado*. The pool had been rimmed with heavy flagstones and at the southern side of the large pool the overflow ran into a smaller pool and the overflow from the smaller pool ran into a shallow ditch that had been paved with flat stones. The ditch coursed south to reach the area behind the ancient church where it had in years past watered a garden that was now a jungle of untended plants and great weeds.

Lee stripped to the buff and walked down to the lower pool, naked as a jaybird except for his dusty hat under which he carried a large bar of laundry soap while he carried his Colt in one hand and his rifle in the other. He placed hat, Colt, and Winchester close at hand as he let himself down in the foot-deep sun-warmed water. "Mother of God," he breathed. It seemed as though his dehydrated body was sucking in the moisture and expanding like a thirsty sponge. He lathered up and then rinsed himself, lazily watching the soap bubbles and the scum drift slowly across the pool to overflow into the dry ditch.

He climbed out of the pool and let the dry wind do his toweling for him. He looked south every now and then, to where he had seen, or imagined, that sudden tiny fleck of light. The moonlight now flooded those naked plains, but there was no sign of life to be seen. Lee dressed himself in clean clothing and dug out a cracked mirror, which he propped on a broken wall so that he might view his face while he trimmed his rough beard. He had never worn a beard while fighting with Lopez. It just might help disguise him, but he really didn't have much faith in it.

Lee picked up his rifle and padded softly down the street toward the old church, now and then peering through a broken window or empty doorway for signs of recent occupancy. It was his big nose that led him to the first sign that someone had recently been in the *poblado*. The odor came through the shattered double doors of the church. Lee walked into the littered nave. Part of the bell tower had crumbled down into the baptistry. Lee padded forward to the sanctuary, following his nose. The stench grew stronger. Someone had recently and fully relieved himself there. "Sacrilegious bastard," said Lee. He found several fresh cigarette butts in the sacristy.

Lee walked up the slight slope of the street back to the pool. The moonlight revealed a place to one side of the larger pool where earth had drifted into a place where the flagging had sunk. He saw heel and sole marks where someone had squatted, likely filling a canteen.

Lee climbed the slope above the pools. He uncased his field glasses and studied the open llano south of the canyon, but there was nothing to be seen out there. The eastern view was the same—nothing but the dreaming emptiness of the low broken hills and the llano beyond them.

Lee swung the glasses to scan the north. The plains

were barren and light-colored under the moon, but something dark stood out on the pale-colored ground. "Sonofabitch!" exclaimed Lee. He ran down to the pool area and picked up one of his two full canteens. He took his rifle and trotted up the canyon road until it trended north to meet the open plains. He set off at a long, swinging stride to the north.

Neither of them moved as Lee came to them with his boots grating on the harsh earth. Leila lay across the saddle with her pretty rump up in the air while Gil lay facedown on the ground with the reins of the roan still held in his left hand. Lee looked back along the level surface of the llano. There was no sign of the claybank horse. Lee raised Leila's head and looked into her sunburned face. She was out completely. Lee pulled her from the saddle and laid her on the ground. He unstoppered the canteen and raised her head with one hand while he held the canteen to her cracked lips. She would not take the water. Lee pulled his scarf from his neck and wet it, then held it between her lips. She nibbled a little at the wet cloth. Lee went to the kid and rolled him onto his back and raised his head. Gil opened his eyes. He grinned as he looked up into Lee's lean, bearded face. "I kinda believed the Devil lived out here in this waterless hell," he husked. "Now I know it."

"Very funny," said Lee dryly. He eyed the kid. "Will you sell me your soul for one drink, kid?"

"Try me," Gil said. He pushed himself up on one elbow and reached eagerly for the canteen. He sipped a little of the blessed water. He looked sideways at Lee. "Didn't think we'd make it, eh, Kershaw?" he asked with half a grin on his sunburned face.

"You didn't," said Lee. "You ain't too bright, kid." He went back to Leila and picked her up. He looked at the kid. "Can you walk?" he asked him.

"How far?" asked Gil.

"Mile and a half."

"There's plenty of water there?"

"Plenty," said Lee. "I even took a bath."

"About time," cracked Gil. He got unsteadily to his feet

with the canteen in his hand. He sipped a little water and looked at Lee as he wiped his mouth. "People were beginning to talk behind your back," he added. "Those that were downwind, of course."

"Of course," agreed Lee. "You've got a great sense of humor, kid."

"My Daddy always thought so."

"How would he know?" asked Lee. "I doubt if he has that one great saving grace—a sense of humor."

Gil nodded. "I'll have to buy that," he admitted.

"Lead out," said Lee. He watched Gil start out, swaying a little in his stride but putting one foot in front of the other with a sort of stolid determination. Lee hoisted Leila back across the saddle, eyed her rounded rump appreciatively, was almost tempted to give it a friendly little pat, and then regretfully shook his head. He led the worn-out roan on after Gil.

Gil gave Lee a hand in getting Leila down from the horse. He placed her on a blanket that Lee had stretched out beside the larger pool. Gil bathed her face and got a little water between her swollen lips. She opened her eyes, looked at Gil, then at the pool of water and then up into the hawk's face of Lee Kershaw. "You must have a divining rod," she cracked.

Lee shook his head. "You and that baby brother of yours would make a great comedy team. It was the dun that found the water. I was heading for the intermittent spring at Ocho Jacales. That's farther east. I had almost forgotten the *poblado* here. Last thing I had heard about it had been that the springs had been plugged up or polluted. I must have trended further west than I figured. It was the dun that saved me."

She raised her head and looked about.

Lee sat down on a rock and felt for the makings. "He's not here," he said. He shaped a cigarette and placed it between Gil's cracked lips. He thumb snatched a lucifer into flame and lighted the cigarette. Gil drew in the smoke. "*Was* he here?" he asked.

Lee nodded as he fashioned a cigarette for himself. "You sure?" asked the kid.

Lee lighted up. He looked down the street. "Go look in the church, but hold your nose," he suggested. "There's not much religion of any kind left in Chad Mercer, if there was ever any in the first place."

"What makes you think it was him?" Leila asked.

Lee shrugged. "No Mexican would have done what he did. Neither would an Apache or a Yaqui."

"Apaches and Yaquis are not religious," challenged Gil.

"They are, kid. Don't ever make the mistake of thinking they are not. Not in our sense, of course. They won't go into a Mexican church except to raid it and loot it. A church like this one would be taboo for them. In any case, none of them would use it for a privy."

"Why wouldn't they go in there?" asked Gil. "Why taboo?"

"Because of the dead," Lee explained. "Maybe more because of the souls of the dead. To them this place is haunted. You're safe enough here from them, especially at night. If they did come around, all you'd have to do is hoot like an owl. That would settle it for them." He grinned. "Bú, the Owl, speaks with the voice of the restless dead, kid. Maybe you'd better practice owl hooting. Handy thing to know. Never know when you might need it."

Gil spat to one side. "You're a great talker, Kershaw. I've heard tell that you can check a pile of horse manure and tell whether it was a white man's horse or an Indian's, and how long it's been there to the hour. Is that how you knew Chad had been around here?"

Lee looked sideways at him. "Now, you don't really expect me to answer that, do you?"

"It would be interesting," Gil answered.

Lee pointed to the set of toe and heel tracks in the soft earth to one side of the pool. "Someone squatted there to drink and fill a canteen," he said.

"How can you be sure it was Chad?" asked Leila.

"Because if it wasn't him, he won't make it to any other water out on the llanos in time to save his life. If he didn't get here or to Ocho Jacales, which is likely dry as a bone about this time of the year, he's likely dead or

89

unconscious from lack of water out on the llano or in the dry hills west of here. *¿Comprende?*" He did not intend to tell them about the spark of light he had seen on the llano south of the canyon mouth.

She nodded. "I understand," she said.

"Hungry?" Lee asked them.

"I can eat," replied Gil eagerly.

"I was sure about that," said Lee dryly. "I was also thinking about your sister."

"Most men usually do," said Gil.

Lee started the fire in the broken-walled adobe. He added another can of beans to the remainder of his meal. He looked up as Gil peered in through a wall gap. "I hope you've got enough sense to know you damned near didn't make it here," he said.

"No thanks to you," said Gil.

Lee stirred the beans. "What the hell do you mean by that?" he asked.

Gil stepped over the broken wall into the room. "We didn't know how bad it was going to be."

Lee shrugged. "I tried to tell you, mister. I've seen stubborn, bullheaded people in my time but nothing quite like you and your sister. I never thought for a minute that the two of you would keep on after me. Hellsfire, kid! I damned near didn't make it myself. I was heading for Ocho Jacales. It was the dun that led me here."

Gil grinned. "So, you admit there's someone smarter than you are, hey, Kershaw?"

"I never argue about that point," Lee admitted. "You can rest here until dusk tomorrow and then start back. You can make that waterhole on the New Mexico side of the line by about dawn. There might be enough water there to get you back to civilization."

Gil shook his head. "It's too risky," he said. "How is it south of here?"

"More of the same, kid."

"You wouldn't lie to me, would you?"

Lee took the bean pot from the fire. "I don't give a good goddamn whether you believe me or not, mister. The

90

point is: you get that sister of yours back to where she belongs. You were beginning to sound like you had some sense back at that last waterhole. You knew what she'd have gotten from those Chiricahua bucks. Over on this side of the line you've got both Apaches and Yaquis and they're broncos, mister! In my professional opinion, I'd rather fight Apaches than Yaquis any day in the week."

"Keep talking," suggested Gil. "You interest me."

"And then there's Lopez," continued Lee. He placed the coffeepot in the embers and looked at Gil. "Lopez goes through the countryside like a plague. The Lopezistas kill, loot, and rape all the time they're shouting: '¡Viva Lopez! Freedom and Justice, or Death!' " Lee picked up the bean pot and walked to the doorway. He paused and looked back at Gil. "If Lopez and his muchachos get a load of your sister with that reddish hair of hers, that creamy skin and green eyes, not to mention that figure of hers, Lopez will have to drive them off with a cocked pistol and spurred boots."

There was a dumb look on the kid's sunburned face. "You mean Lopez himself would protect her? I don't get it."

Lee rolled his eyes upward. "You *are* stupid! Listen! As long as Lopez wanted her first, he'd kill any one of his muchachos that tried to get at her. But Lopez gets tired of any woman, even a woman like your sister, in a hurry, amigo. After he was through with her, his lieutenants would shake dice for her each night until they were through with her and then she'd be booted out naked in front of the mob."

"Not if Chad Mercer was there!" cried Gil. "None of them would dare to touch her!"

Lee shook his head in patient resignation to facts. "I thought you had more sense than that, kid." He jerked his head. "Now get outside and stand guard while I feed your sister."

Leila was sitting up beside the pool combing her long unbraided hair while she looked into Lee's cracked pocket mirror. The moonlight shone on her, softening her sunburned skin and cracked lips. "Did you and Gil get every-thing settled?" she asked.

"¿Quién sabe?" he asked as he filled her plate.

"You might as well know," she said. "He'll do as I ask him to do."

He squatted beside her. "You mean what you *tell* him to do," he corrected.

She shrugged. "Either way."

"The bigger the damned fool he," said Lee.

"I'll go on alone!" she snapped.

"Then you're a bigger damned fool than he is," said Lee. "You just don't know this country, missy."

"Mexico is civilized," she retorted.

"Sure, sure," he agreed. "But not where Lopez is."

She slanted her great green eyes sideways at him. "You're just trying to frighten me," she accused.

He shook his head. "I doubt if I can frighten either you or that brother of yours."

She finished her beans and looked down the street toward the moonlighted church and its broken bell tower. "Why did these people leave?" she asked.

Lee finished shaping a cigarette. He placed it between his lips while he felt for a match. "Go look behind the church," he suggested. "A Campo Santo can almost al-ways tell the answer to a question like that."

"The Campo Santo?"

He nodded as he lighted up. "The graveyard. About seventy-five percent of the graves there are of adult males that died in the last twenty-five years or so."

"So?" she asked. "How did they die?"

He lighted the cigarette. "Apaches and Yaquis," he said. He squatted on his heels and looked thoughtfully down the moonlighted street. "I've seen some of these *poblados* with no male under fifty years or over ten years of age and no young women at all."

"Why?" she asked curiously.

He blew a perfect smoke ring and watched it drift across the pool. "The Apaches and Yaquis don't take adult male white prisoners. They figure they can raise those who are under ten years into their ways. I don't have to tell you what happened to the young women." He glanced sideways at her. "And then there's always Lopez," he added.

"He came here?"

Lee nodded. "The place was on the decline even then. Years past there were mines in those hills west of here. There was a time when the *camino* came through here and there was much traffic to the north. They had great hopes. The mines began to peter out. The Apaches and Yaquis grew bolder. They stopped the traffic across the Llanos de Carretas. The *poblado* began to sink into decay, but there were still some hundreds of people here." He shrugged. "There was no future here, but it was home to them. Then Lopez came. That was five years ago."

"You were with him?" she asked.

He shook his head. "Not that time. It seems as though the Federales were looking for Lopez, and he was hiding in the hills west of here. The people here made the mistake of telling the Federales where Lopez was hiding. He barely escaped with his life and lost many of his men. It took him a year to get back onto his feet as a professional *revolutionario*. There was a small Federale garrison here. Lopez sent a small part of his force to draw them off into the hills and the dust had hardly settled when he rode into the *poblado* with his muchachos." Lee's voice died away. He looked thoughtfully at his cigarette. "One of his boys told me the story a few years back—with gestures and much laughter." He shook his head.

"Was Chad with Lopez at that time?"

He looked down the long moonlighted street.

"Lee?" she asked.

He looked sideways at her. "Ask him when you find him," he suggested. He stood up and walked down the street toward the church.

Gil met Lee at the church door. "He was here all right," he said.

Lee grinned. "You check that pile of crap for sign, kid?"

Gil shook his head. He held out a big hand. Cupped in the palm was a brass tobacco canteen. The initials C.R.M. had been embossed on the metal. "Fancy," said Lee.

"Chadwick Robert Mercer," said Gil. "Leila gave this canteen to him not more than two months ago."

Lee looked up at him. "Now you *know* you must go on," he murmured. "You and sis. Heroic to the bitter end."

"Shit!" snapped Gil.

Lee leaned against the church wall and looked south. "Ten miles south of here is a branch line of the local stagecoach route. It only runs when the Yaquis are quiet, but even then it usually has an escort of Rurales. You two can make it to that line by taking turns riding the roan. You can flag down a coach when you get there. It can take you into Galeana on the Rio Santa Maria. From Galeana you can get to Ojo Laguna or Villa Ahumado on the main highway between Chihuahua City and Ciudad Juarez and take the stage north to Juarez. Then all you have to do is to cross the Rio Grande into El Paso."

"What about you?" asked Gil.

"I came here on business," replied Lee. "That business is still unfinished."

Gil studied Lee. "If we get to Galeana, we can report to the Rurales that you're in Mexico."

"Go ahead," said Lee. "By the time you get to Galeana, I'll be somewhere else."

"Maybe Chad is in Galeana," suggested the kid.

Lee shook his head. "Not likely. He'll keep away from such places until he finds Lopez."

"You're sure of that, eh?"

Lee looked at the kid. "What do you mean, kid?"

"Maybe Lopez is in Galeana."

"Then, you'd better keep your beloved sister to hell out of there!" Lee walked back up the street.

"You want me to stand first guard?" called out Gil.

Lee looked back at him. "The Apaches and Yaquis won't come here at night," he reminded Gil.

"You're sure about that?"

"Just hoot like an owl if they do," said Lee. "You ought to be good at that. Get some sleep, kid. I am. It'll be a long day tomorrow for all of us."

Leila had spread out her blankets in a jacal near the pools. "Was Chad here?" she asked over her shoulder as Lee stood within the doorway.

"He was," replied Lee. "He left a memento. Nice little brass tobacco canteen embossed with his initials. Maybe if he thinks enough of it, he'll come back for it."

There was no sign from her that she understood his meaning. She sat down on her blankets and pulled off her scuffed boots. "You'll never catch him now," she said. "He's got too good a lead."

"So you can go on and meet him somewhere and be happy forever after?" he asked.

She tilted her head to one side. "Do you always think like that?"

"Only when I'm dealing with you and your baby brother," he replied.

She lay back and locked her hands together at the nape of her neck. "What did Chad ever do to you to make you hate him so?"

He shook his head. "I don't hate him," he said.

"You must! You're risking your own life to come into Mexico after him."

"It's my job," he said.

"You could have refused Dad," she said.

"And lose the Querencia?" he asked.

She studied him as Gil had studied him shortly before he had come to the jacal. "Does the Querencia mean that much to you? That you'd track down a man who was once your best friend so that you can hold the Querencia?"

He shrugged. "It's as good a reason as any."

"But not the real reason?" she queried.

Lee felt for his tobacco canteen. "You're very sociable tonight," he remarked.

She sat up and placed her back against the wall. "You're lonely," she suddenly accused. "You're *always* lonely! That's why you came back to the Querencia! That's why you keep old Anselmo Campos with you on the Querencia."

"That's why I'm hunting down Chad Mercer," he quietly added.

She was puzzled. She shook her head. "You've guessed wrong a good part of your life, Lee. The years you spent away from home, wandering from one place to another, hunting men against whom you had nothing personal, fighting revolutions in which you had no personal interest. And, in the end, you were always alone."

He lighted the cigarette. He shoved back his hat and studied her. "You're quite the student of human nature," he said dryly.

Her eyes flicked back and forth as she studied his hawk's face and hard blue eyes for a real clue as to his outlook on life, but she found nothing there. "It's the game, isn't it?" she asked at last. "One man against another; the hunter and the hunted. You really don't care whether or not Chad murdered Frank, do you?"

"I liked Frank," he admitted.

"But you liked Chad better!" she cried.

"It's my job," he said defensively.

"But you've been thinking of yourself as a rancher, Lee."

Lee smiled wryly. "I was about to figure out that I had made a mistake in that."

Leila brushed back her lovely loose hair in a gesture so utterly feminine that Lee felt a flow of emotion within him that he had not experienced in a long time. "How much is Dad paying you?" she asked.

"A thousand for the first week. Five hundred each week thereafter," he replied.

"You could drag out the hunt a long time," she suggested.

He shook his head. "I deliver the goods as quickly as I can."

"Goods?" she asked incredulously.

He waved a hand. "A man, if you will."

She nodded quickly. "I *will!* Look, Lee, Gil and I have plenty of money. Enough to pay you for your trouble with something besides. Forget about Chad. You won't catch him anyway."

Lee did not speak. He took the cigarette from his lips.

"You can go back to the Querencia," she added. "You can pay off Dad with the money we give you."

Lee flipped the cigarette into the fireplace. "Get some sleep," he said. "You'll need it for tomorrow."

"I'm not going back," she said firmly.

He turned on a heel and left the jacal.

Lee spread out his light tarp and blanket on a softer patch of ground not too far behind the Campo Santo with the dun tethered to a scrub tree. He could hear Gil and his sister talking now and then as the wind shifted a little, but he couldn't distinguish what they were saying. Lee untethered the dun and looped the reins about his left arm. He lay down on his bed. The dun would stand as long as the reins were about Lee's arm. Lee dozed as the moon waned and died to be followed by the velvety darkness. The wind died away and complete silence came over the old *poblado*.

Lee suddenly raised his head. He rolled over onto his lean belly. Something moved along the wall of the Campo Santo. Lee loosed the reins and let them lie on the ground to hold the dun where he was standing. Lee worked his way over a crumbled part of the cemetery wall and squatted close beside a sagging mausoleum.

Something grated on the ground beyond the wall. Lee stood up and as he did so he heard something move near the back of the church. He faded into the thicker darkness of the church wall and skirted it until he reached the front of the church. He entered it and walked softly through it to the rear door that opened into the sacristy. A shadow passed in front of the doorless opening. Lee moved like a hunting cat. His left arm encircled Leila's waist while his hard right hand clamped over her mouth. He looked expectantly beyond her to the wall of the Campo Santo.

The dun whinnied sharply. There was a harsh scuffling

of boots and hoofs on the hard ground. The dun reared and threw himself sideways. Gil cursed savagely. He staggered back through the break in the wall.

"Get to hell away from my horse!" ordered Lee.

Gil turned sideways and crouched a little.

"Let go that Colt," ordered Lee. "I've got your sister here, bub. Come on over here! With your hands up!"

Gil walked slowly toward the rear of the church. As he came closer they could see the blood running down the side of his face. "That gawddamned dun bites like a lobo!" he snapped.

Lee grinned. "He's part watchdog," said Lee.

"Indian fashion!" accused Gil. "Damned if I don't think you're a breed at that!"

Lee raised his head a little. "You know better than that," he said quietly. He took Leila's Colt from its holster and then released her.

"Now what?" asked Gil as he wiped the blood from his face.

"Like I said: flag down a coach on the Galeana Road and go from there to the Chihuahua Highway," replied Lee. "This is the last time I am going to tell you. If you leave a couple of hours before sunrise and travel southeast, you can make the Galeana Road by midmorning."

"What about you?" asked Gil.

Lee reached over and took Gil's Colt from its holster. "I'm leaving here as soon as I can," he said. "Now, listen, and listen well! I want no more interference from you two! I've told you that before, but this is absolutely the last time! Now, keep to hell out of my way, mister, unless you want to come shooting!"

Lee walked back through the darkness to the pools. He took the two rifles and walked back to the church. He emptied all four weapons. He led the dun back to the pool and watered him. He could hear the two Luscombes moving about in the darkness beyond the second pool. Lee hooked his full canteens to his saddle. He got the roan mare and saddled it and then he placed the emptied pistols in a saddlebag and sheathed one of the empty

Winchesters. He thrust the other beneath a saddle strap and then led both horses down the street. He knew the two Luscombes were watching him from the deep shadows.

A mile south of the *poblado* he loosed the roan mare and slapped her hard on the rump. She obediently trotted back toward the *poblado*. Lee rode hard for fifteen minutes and then dismounted. He cut a chew of Wedding Cake and stuffed it into his mouth. He looked back toward the dimness of the low hills about the canyon of the *poblado*. He spat sideways, wiped his mouth with the back of a hand, and then grinned. "That nervy young sonofabitch," he said. He led the dun to the south and west.

TWELVE

IT WAS THE LONE *zopilote* that bothered Lee Kershaw. He had seen it about midday, hovering in the sky like a scrap of charred paper caught in the updraft from a chimney. The buzzard hung in the sky over the low hills to the west of the faint rutted road that led to Pedregosa in the western mountains. There was something dead or dying in those empty hills. Lee wiped the sweat from his face as he debated his choices. He was already halfway through his second canteen and he didn't know of any waterholes in those hills. There was water further along the Pedregosa Road, but it was twenty miles to the southwest. Common sense told him to go on to that water, of which he could be sure, rather than to risk going into those heat-baked hills where there probably wasn't any water. Still . . . that *zopilote*.

Lee mounted the dun and rode toward the hills. In a

gap he found a fresh cigarette butt. He looked up into the blazing sky. The *zopilote* was still there. "Don't look at *me,* you bastard!" cried Lee.

The dun whinnied and quickened his pace. Lee dismounted and drew his Winchester from its sheath. He led the dun forward. A fragment of eroded wall caught his eye. Beyond it was a *bosquecillo* of dusty trees. Lee halted. He eye-scouted the area. There was no sound, no sign of life. He looked up at the sky. The *zopilote* was veering off on the wind. He swung back, a little lower this time, and floated right over Lee and then two hundred feet high.

The dun whinnied and trotted forward. Lee let him go. He followed him. The dun rounded the eroded ruins. Lee walked to the roofless ruin and looked across the broken walls. The dun was drinking. Lee crawled over the wall into the debris-choked interior of the ruins and walked to the gaping doorway. He looked through it toward the dusty trees. A pair of bare feet showed from beneath the brush. Lee padded forward. Nothing moved. He parted the brush with his rifle barrel and looked into the staring eyes of a dead man. The body, clad only in baggy underwear, was already starting to swell in the great heat, but the man had not been dead long; perhaps he had died earlier that day or late the night before. Lee rolled him over. He quickly turned his head away. The back of the skull had been shattered by a large-caliber bullet and the gaping, blood-encrusted hole was alive with buzzing flies.

Lee walked to the waterhole. It was almost dry. Many tracks showed in the wide margin of dried mud about the green-scummed water. Lee slapped the dun on the rump to move him out of the way. There were worn boot tracks in the mud and the tracks of a horse. Lee stood up and shaped a cigarette. He eyed the area as he did so. The sun glinted from something lying near the side wall of the ruin. He went to it. It was a freshly fired brass cartridge case, caliber .44/40.

Lee looked over the low wall of the roofless ruin. Boot marks showed in the loose dirt along with several cigarette butts. He began to reconstruct the scene. A man lying patiently in wait in the ruins while another man rode up to the waterhole. One shot had killed him. The spent cartridge had been ejected over the wall. The ambusher had stripped off the dead man's clothing and had taken his horse.

Lee walked back to the dead man. Beyond him he found a pair of heavy saddlebags. Lee whistled softly. The bags were stamped with the letters and insignia of the Mexican Postal Service. He opened the bags. The mail was still contained within them, but every letter and package had been ripped open. "Looking for money, the sonofabitch," said Lee quietly.

Lee walked through the *bosquecillo*. Hoof tracks showed on the soft earth. Whoever had murdered the mail courier had taken his clothing as well as his horse. Lee looked up at the *zopilote*. "I'll screw you," he said.

He dragged the body to the ruins and placed it in a low spot. He dumped rubbish over it and then kicked at the weak wall until it tumbled in over the grave. "Rest in peace," he murmured.

Lee led the dun south while he constructed a mental map of the area ahead of him. Directly southeast the only place of habitation would be San Pedro de Arriba, while further southeast would be Casas Grandes and Malpaís. South of Malpaís was the little placita of Onate and a few miles beyond that was Galeana. At Galeana the stagecoach route went eastward to the Chihuahua Highway.

For two miles beyond the dying waterhole he tracked the murderer by finding bits of dried mud that had been cast off by the horse's hoofs to lie on the sterile ground. By the time he had found the last bits of mud, the trail trended toward Onate, and not toward Pedregosa in the mountains to the west.

The distant yellow lights winked through the darkness like the eyes of a pack of hunting cougars. Lee turned in his saddle to look back through the darkness. It was an hour before moonrise. He might have passed his quarry in the darkness, but knowing Chad Mercer as he now did,

Lee's only indication of having passed Mercer would have been a bullet crashing through his back.

The wind had shifted with the coming of the cooler night air and it brought with it the impelling aroma of resinous woodsmoke mingled with the tantalizing odor of cooking beans rich in chile sauce. "Mother of God," breathed Lee. He stood up in his sweat-damp saddle and eased his weary crotch as he reached the first outlying jacales of Onate. A cur leaped eagerly toward Lee and the dun, baring his teeth and laying back his chewed up ears. "Get back, you mangy sonofabitch!" cried Lee. "I've come to fight for Lopez!"

Lee dismounted outside of a cantina and hat-slapped the dust from his clothing. He removed his moccasins and replaced them with his boots. Those mocs would make any Mexican look with thick suspicion on a Yanqui who wore them. Lee took his rifle from the scabbard, slanted his hat lower over his telltale blue eyes, then pushed open the door of the cantina. The heavenly odor of succulent beans swimming in rich red-eyed grease was coupled with that of freshly made tacos. Mingled with the aroma of the food was the sharper odor of tequila slops and sweat, both ancient and modern, with the faintest touch of manure added for piquancy. "Viva Mexico," murmured Lee to himself as he walked to the end of the zinc-topped counter. He leaned his rifle against the wall close at his right side. He felt for his tobacco canteen as he looked through the thick-rifted tobacco smoke. Two men were seated at a table hunched over their food, rapidly spooning up the rich chile beans with scoop-shaped pieces of crisp tortillas. Another man stood at the far end of the bar moodily staring into an empty tequila glass.

The bartender lumbered toward Lee. "Good evening, señor. Your pleasure, sir?"

Lee slipped easily into his excellent Spanish. "Good evening to you, Tomás Castanoa," he replied. "Brandy and food, if you please."

Tomás Castanoa stared at Lee with his one eye. "For the love of God," he breathed. He hastily looked back over his shoulder, then turned and leaned closer to Lee. "You are traveling under your own name?" he asked.

Lee shrugged. "Is that dangerous here in Onate?"

Tomás waggled his head. "Not at present. The Rurales were here yesterday on their way north to escort the stagecoach south to Galeana."

"When is that stage due here?" asked Lee.

"Within two hours. They do not stop here as a rule." Tomás eyed Lee. "Your beard fooled me, old friend, but those eyes—*never!*"

"There is brandy?" asked Lee.

Tomás waved both hands. "Baconora, Jerez, or Pride of Chihuahua?"

"Baconora," said Lee. He grinned. "Did you say Pride of Chihuahua?"

Tomás grinned back. "Burro piss for the peons. I myself drink only Baconora."

"Get it, then," suggested Lee. He shaped a cigarette.

Tomás got the bottle. He glanced at Lee. "Viva Lopez," he said tentatively in a low voice.

"Freedom and Justice, or Death," replied Lee.

Tomás filled two glasses and sadly shook his head. "I can no longer ride with the hero Lopez," he said.

Lee stared uncomprehendingly at the Mexican. *"You?* The 'Hero of El Corralitos'? The 'Right Arm of Lopez'?"

Tomás waved a deprecating hand. "I but did my duty at El Corralitos," said Tomás modestly.

Lee looked at the others in the cantina. "Those others," he asked. "Do they have the big ears?"

"They will not talk. They know better. I will get your food." Tomás waddled back into the kitchen.

Lee lighted his cigarette. It had been two years since Lee himself had ridden with Lopez, but before that time Tomás Castanoa, loaded with honors and pesos, had retired from being a professional *revolutionario* to open his cantina in Onate.

Tomás waddled back along behind the bar. He placed on the bar a huge bowl of chile beans thick with reddish, oily liquid upon which floated large globules of melting fat that seemed to look up at Lee with iridescent but unseeing eyes. Tomás placed a plate of tortillas beside the bowl. "My own dinner, amigo," he said with a smile.

"It would be a shame to eat it, Tomás One-Eye," murmured Lee. "It is a work of art."

"There is more," replied Tomás. He shoved the bottle of Baconora so that it was close at hand. "You will ride again with Lopez?" he asked.

Lee shrugged as he scooped up the beans with a fold of warm tortilla. "Who knows? Is Lopez getting ready to ride once again?"

"Who knows?" questioned Tomás in turn. "You will be here for a time?"

"I have business elsewhere," replied Lee.

Tomás studied him knowingly. "Then you *have* heard from Lopez, eh?"

"Indirectly," replied Lee. He looked up at Tomás. "Is he gathering his men together at the old rendezvous?"

"Perhaps. It is so rumored. I, myself, do not really know. It is rumored, with good authority, that this time Lopez will be victorious."

"He has tried many times," Lee said dryly.

"He has many new guns and many new recruits."

Lee shoved back the empty bowl. He felt for the makings. "Such as?" he queried.

"Your compañero Chad Mercer. He was here not more than two hours past."

Lee shrugged. "I can catch up with him."

"He had been riding hard, but then it is quite evident that you have as well. I took the liberty of looking at your horse while I was back in the kitchen. Perhaps you both left the States in a hurry?"

Lee grinned crookedly. "Don't we always?"

Tomás filled the glasses. "And you, you gained nothing from the old days?" he asked solicitously.

"Such as?" asked Lee.

Tomás waved a hand to encompass the cantina. "This is *my* freedom and justice gained by fighting with Lopez. Have you nothing left, my friend, that you should again risk your life?"

Lee lighted his cigarette and held out open hands. "Money comes easily and goes faster," he said.

Tomás nodded knowingly. "And Lopez pays well the Yanqui gunfighters, eh?"

The sonofabitch still owes me from the last time, thought Lee.

Tomás eyed his drink. "Your friend Chad Mercer risked a great deal by riding into Galeana," he said. "Something was bothering him." Tomás looked directly at Lee. "He had little time to talk. He traded his horse for one of mine and rode quickly on. I warned him about the Rurales, but he would not listen." Tomás hesitated. "There is more. That horse he rode here as well as the clothing he was wearing belong to a man of Galeana. A mail courier by the name of Juan Vidal who rides with mail from Galeana to Pedregosa. Juan Vidal should have passed through here this evening on his way back to Galeana. One wonders where Juan Vidal is now."

Lee shrugged. He downed his drink and refilled the glass.

"But, then, a mail courier is a Federale," continued Tomás. "If Lopez rides again, and Chad Mercer rides with him, it will be war against the Federales. Therefore one must consider Juan Vidal as a Federale, for was he not employed by the government?"

"Wonderful logic," said Lee dryly. He looked at Tomás. "But why did Chad Mercer ride into Galeana?"

Tomas quickly shifted his one eye. "The stagecoach passes through here after moonrise," he said. "Get your horse out of the street, for perhaps the Rurales might get curious about him."

"I'll need another horse," said Lee.

"I have a good gray," suggested Tomás. "Come with me, amigo."

Lee picked up his rifle and followed the cantina owner through to the kitchen and then out behind the building. The gray was in a corral. Lee liked the looks of the rangy horse.

"Listen!" cried Tomás. "The stagecoach! It is early!"

The steady tattoo of many hoofbeats came from the road to the north.

Lee ran quickly between the cantina and the building next to it. He untethered the dun and led him back between the buildings and then slapped him on the dusty rump. The dun trotted back toward the corral to commune with the gray. Lee pulled his hat low over his eyes and stood in the shadow of the cantina. The pounding rhythm of the hoofs mingled with the pistollike cracking of the whip filled the street. The coach was being driven fast. Two horsemen pounded ahead of it. Their dark sombreroes had the gilt snake and eagle insignia of Mexico on their fronts and the dark uniforms identified them as Rurales. The stage rolled swiftly toward the cantina with six red-mouthed mules doing their damnedest as the whip cracked incessantly over their heads. Lee saw a young woman peering from a window of the coach. A dusty roan horse had been tethered to the rear of the coach. Then the stage raced past with a whining of wheels and a clucking of sandboxes and was gone in a swirling of yellow dust. Through the dust pounded six more Rurales riding with their carbine butts resting against their right hips.

"They are in much of the hurry," observed Tomás from behind Lee.

"Why?" asked Lee.

"They are carrying the payroll for the mines in the Sierra del Arco," replied Tomás.

"That is why they have the Rurale guard?"

"That is a fact," agreed Tomás.

"And Lopez has many new recruits and many new guns but no money for his war chest, eh?"

Tomás nodded.

"How far is Lopez from Galeana?" Lee asked.

Tomás smiled secretively. "It is not for me to say."

"And the soldiers that garrison Galeana? They are there at this time?"

Tomás inspected his fingernails. "They have gone south on information that Lopez has raided a ranch down there for horses and mules."

"Christamighty!" said Lee. That was Leila Luscombe

he had seen in the Galeana coach. She was going into Galeana; Chad Mercer was already there; the Federales had left the town unguarded; Lopez could not be far off.

Lee ran back to his two horses. He shifted his saddle. "Trade me hats, amigo," he said over his shoulder.

"I will give you the gift for old times' sake," replied Tomás. He went into the cantina and brought out a heavy sombrero with a coin silver band. He handed it to Lee. Lee held out his own good Stetson to Tomás, but the cantina owner shook his head. Lee stowed the Stetson in a saddlebag.

"It was good to see you, amigo," said Tomás. "The Heroes of El Corralitos! We two together, eh?"

Lee shook his head. "*You,* my old companion, are the *only* hero of El Corralitos."

Tomás nodded with modesty. "I know it," he admitted. "But at least we two were there together, riding boot to boot while fighting with Lopez."

"Viva Lopez!" cried Lee as he mounted.

"Freedom and Justice, or Death!" replied Tomás.

"Viva Lopez!" repeated Lee as he rode between the two buildings to the one street of Onate leading the dun.

"Go with God, amigo!" shouted Tomás.

Lee nodded. He waved a hand as he turned into the street. "I may need him before tonight is out," he said to himself. He let the gray run as he reached the end of the straggling town. Far ahead of Lee was a thin swirling of dust rising in the night air, and beyond that he could see the faint, winking lights of Galeana.

THIRTEEN

LEE CAME INTO Galeana by a side road, avoiding the better-traveled road from Onate. He rode through narrow, dusty streets where men looked at him sideways from under the brims of their sombreroes. The wind brought the faint sound of guitars from the direction of the plaza. Lee dismounted outside of a ramshackle livery stable. A smiling boy came to meet him.

"I want to keep these horses here only a little while," said Lee. "Where is your father, boy?"

"He has gone to El Carmen to trade for mules. He will not be back until late tomorrow."

Lee nodded as he shaped a cigarette. "Do not unsaddle the gray," he instructed. "Rub down the dun and feed him a little. Do not give either of them too much water."

The boy nodded. He looked into the cold blue Yanqui eyes. "Is it possible that you might want these horses in a hurry?" he asked.

"You're getting the idea," replied Lee as he lighted the cigarette. He placed it between the lips of the boy. "There is a silver dollar in it for you, little friend," said Lee. "You understand?"

"Thanks," said the boy. He winked knowingly.

"For nothing," replied Lee. He watched the boy lead the two horses into the stable. The boy looked back over his shoulder. "You ride for Lopez?" he asked.

Lee shook his head. "I ride alone, little friend."

"Your secret is safe with me," suggested the boy.

"My *secret*, if I *have* one, boy, is safe only with *me*," said Lee quietly. "Why did you ask me if I rode with Lopez?"

The boy expertly blew a smoke ring. "Lopez always needs gunfighters from the north. A man such as yourself. Your profession shows plainly, mister. There was a man here several hours ago. A man such as yourself. He was in the plaza. It is said he once rode with Lopez."

"A man with light hair and mustache. Perhaps a little taller than I am? He has good teeth that he shows when he smiles, eh?"

"Yes. He rode a fine sorrel. My father once owned that sorrel but sold him to Tomás One-Eye of Onate."

Lee fashioned a cigarette for himself. "How do you know that he once rode with Lopez?"

The boy winked. "Both you and I know Lopez is nearby, eh, mister? There are some men of Lopez here in Galeana now that the soldiers have left. You, yourself, have not fooled me, mister."

Lee lighted up. "Where does the southbound stage stop here in Galeana?" he asked.

"At the Hotel Royal," replied the boy.

Lee handed the boy a dollar. "One keeps his word, eh, little friend?" His cold blue eyes held the dark ones of the lad for a moment and then he walked to the door. He walked to the plaza and along the south side of it under the wilted, dusty shade trees. A mule brayed hoarsely from the stagecoach station on the east side of the plaza next to the hotel. Lee cut across the plaza and stopped beside the bandstand. Hostlers were leading fresh mules to the dusty Abbott-Downing Concord coach while others led off the dusty team that had hauled the stagecoach from the north. The boot was being unloaded. Gil Luscombe held the reins of the roan mare that had been tethered behind the coach. Leila walked out of the hotel and toward the coach. Gil spoke to her and then led the tired roan to a livery stable that was adjacent to the station. Then the two Luscombes went into the hotel.

Lee crossed quickly to the north side of the plaza and glanced toward the hotel. A tall man was walking quickly toward the alleyway behind the hotel. Lee walked swiftly toward the opposite side of the hotel through the busy livery and stagecoach yard. One Rurale leaned against a railing while fashioning a cigarette. The others were not in sight, but their dusty mounts were hitched to a rail in front of the stagecoach office. The lone Rurale did not even look up as Lee reached the alleyway. The alleyway was dark, shadowed from the bright moonlight by a long warehouse that stood on the opposite side of the alley from the hotel.

Lee quickly eased into a doorway as a foot squelched in the alley filth fifty feet away. He rested his hand on the butt of his Colt. He didn't want to shoot. The whole *poblado* would be down about his ears if he did so. The local police would more than likely have a good likeness of Lee Kershaw on their "wanted" posters.

A tall figure seemed to swim into view through the darkness. The man stopped and looked up at the second floor of the hotel. A window slid up and a shade was let roll upward. Yellow lamplight struck the lean, bearded face of Chad Mercer. "Put out that damned light!" he snarled. The light flicked out. Boots squelched in the filth. Chad looked back over his shoulder. The muzzle of the six-gun probed hard into his lean gut just above the belt buckle. Chad slowly turned his head. "*¿Quien es?*" he asked. "*¿Amigo?*"

"Amigo, shit!" said Lee. "Don't move, mister!"

Chad grinned. "It took you long enough, Lee," he said.

"You had some help," replied Lee.

"I'll bet Old Man Luscombe would shit if he knew about it," said Chad. "What happens now, Lee? Surely you don't think you can get me quietly out of Galeana, do you? Lopez knows I'm here and he knows I aim to ride with him again. You haven't got a chance to get me out of here, Lee. Come on! Forget it! I'll buy you a drink."

The Colt hammer sear clicked. "The warrant says dead or alive, Chad," said Lee.

"So? You kill me and you'll never get out of Galeana alive, Lee."

"I'll chance that," said Lee.

Chad looked steadily at Lee. "What about *her*?" he softly asked.

"A helluva lot you care about that woman," replied

Lee. "When you dumped that rattlesnake nest of Chirica-huas down on us, you knew she and the kid were with me. You know how close that one was? Hombre, I could smell death above my own stink every second I was legging it back to my horse. God alone knows how the two of them got away."

Chad laughed softly. "They likely had you to cover for them. Good ol' Lee Kershaw!"

"I was thinking about *myself* at the time."

"Sometimes I almost believe that hardcase front of yours, Lee."

"Stop talking," ordered Lee. "I've got two horses four blocks from here. Now you and me are going to take a nice little *paseo* through the horseshit in these alleyways until we get to those horses. You'll have a sore ass by day-break, hombre. I've only got one saddle."

Mercer's head moved a little. Lee turned sideways and laid the barrel of his Colt right alongside Gil Luscombe's skull just above his left ear. The kid went down without a sound. Lee glanced down the dimly lit rear hallway of the hotel. Leila Luscombe was standing there.

"Move!" snapped Lee at Mercer. "*¡Andale!*"

"You won't get away with this," repeated Chad. He looked into Lee's hard eyes and *moved*. They reached a cross alleyway. They turned up it to reach the plaza sidewalk. Lee looked to the right to see Leila standing in front of the hotel watching them. "She makes one move to help you, hombre," warned Lee, "and so help me Christ I'll cut your backbone in half with a bullet."

"Get back, Leila!" called out Chad.

A sound rose above the quiet murmuring of the leaves and the guitars. It was the hard hoof thudding of many horses being ridden at speed into the plaza. A man yelled. A bugle blew raggedly. A gun exploded at the rear of the stagecoach station corral. A high-pitched yelling arose above the pounding of the hoofs and the cracking of gunshots. Lee knew that type of yelling. He had done it many times himself. "Jesus Christ!" he said. "Lopez!"

Chad grinned. "In the nick of time, hombre!"

Horsemen pounded past them. One of them leaned

111

from his saddle and hooked an arm about Leila Luscombe to lift her easily and dump her across his thighs. He slapped her rump hard and screamed with laughter as he swept past the stagecoach station. Gunfire broke out from the side of the plaza opposite the stagecoach station.

Lee gripped Chad by the collar and propelled him back down the alleyway to the one that ran along behind the hotel. Three horsemen pounded toward them. A door swung open and yellow lamplight flooded about Lee and Chad. "Santiago!" yelled Chad. "It's me! Chad Mercer! Help me, compañero!"

"It's the Yanqui gunfighter, Captain Santiago!" yelled one of the riders. He pointed his rifle at Lee. Lee rolled over a low wall and landed ankle-deep in loose filth. Chickens scattered out from beneath his pounding feet as he ran toward a passageway. A gun exploded behind him. Something plucked at his left sleeve. "Run, you sonofabitch!" yelled Chad Mercer in sheer delight.

Lee burst out onto the plaza right in front of a group of horsemen. A gun exploded right beside his head, half deafening him. A horse slammed him sideways across a low hedge into a small yard. He went to earth and lay still, peering under the dusty hedge. Glass shattered behind him as a bullet smashed through a front window. Smoke was already wreathing up from the front of the Hotel Royal. A bright tongue of flame leaped from a shattered window and licked hungrily at the window frame. A burning curtain floated across the street and alighted among the dry leaves of a tree. A bell began to slam back and forth.

"Viva Lopez!" screamed a horseman. "Liberty and Justice, or Death! Viva Lopez!" He punctuated the cry by hurling an empty bottle through a hotel window.

There was a sharp crackling of gunfire at the stagecoach station as though some giant were ripping heavy canvas in successive jerks. The sound of the bell became wilder and more strident. A woman screamed through the swirling smoke.

Lee raised his head. A man was leading the mule team of the stagecoach out into the street. The right-hand wheels of the coach bumped over the sprawled body of a Rurale. Another man swung up into the driver's seat and expertly threaded the reins through his fingers. Three rifle-carrying men clambered atop the coach. A young woman was pushed toward the coach and through an open door into the interior of it. The door was slammed shut behind her. It was Leila Luscombe.

A tall man ran through the smoke. He held a rifle in his hands. He looked toward where Lee was hidden and pointed his rifle in that direction. "Mercer, you sonofabitch," murmured Lee. He bellied through the tall dry grass of the yard and pushed open the door of the house. He crawled in and shut the door behind him. The house was quiet. A lamp guttered on a table. Lee bolted the door and ran through the house to the kitchen. Loud voices came from the front of the house. A rifle butt thudded against the door. Lee stepped out into the backyard. A dog launched himself at Lee. A hooked bootheel caught him in the throat and the heavy barrel of the Colt smashed in his skull. Lee kicked the lifeless body aside and went over the back wall just as he heard voices in the kitchen.

The warehouse across the alleyway from the hotel was in flames. A door gaped open on the alleyway. Lee plunged through the doorway into the thick swirling smoke. He ran toward the front of the warehouse through a pattering rain of embers that burned through his clothing and seared his flesh. He coughed and his eyes began to stream. He threw a shoulder against the locked front door of the warehouse and smashed through to the street just as the warehouse roof collapsed into the interior, sending up a billowing cloud of smoke, flame, and incandescent gas.

Lee legged it down a deserted street through the swirling smoke and fiery rain of embers. He glanced sideways up a cross alleyway and saw the stagecoach go rocketing past, followed by a heavy escort of yelling Lopezistas. Lee caught a glimpse of the pale face of Leila Luscombe framed in a window of the coach.

Lee made his way toward the livery stable through a tangle of crooked side streets and alleys. It was a cinch that Mercer would not stay in Galeana now. He had obviously cast his lot with Lopez. The boy met Lee at the opened door of the livery stable. "I *knew* you rode with Lopez," he said with a wide grin.

Lee started toward the gray.

"That's more than Lopez knows," a quiet voice said from behind Lee.

Lee whirled. Gil Luscombe stood there. "Your amigo Mercer is gone," said Lee coldly. "They've taken your sister with them. How come they forgot about *you*, bub?"

"I'll need a horse, bub," replied Gil.

"The dun is worn thin," said Lee.

Gil nodded. He looked at the boy. "I want a saddled horse, muchacho," he said. "A good one. You understand?"

"The very best, señor," replied the boy. He ran to get the mount.

Lee leaned against a post and made a cigarette. "What's your game, Gil?" he quietly asked.

"They took my sister," replied Gil.

Lee shrugged. "She's with her dearly beloved," he said.

"It's not funny!" snapped Gil.

Lee lighted his cigarette. "So, you've finally gotten around to figuring that out, eh?"

"You damned near fractured my skull back there at the hotel," accused Gil.

Lee shook his head. "Not unless I had wanted to," he said.

"You still going after Mercer?" demanded the kid.

Lee nodded. "And I don't need any help, bub."

"You've got a conceit like a braying jackass, bub," said Gil.

"You say such nice things," Lee murmured. He looked over his shoulder. "Give him that chestnut, boy."

"The pinto is a better horse, mister," replied the boy.

"No pinto has guts," said Lee. "You know that, boy."

The boy shrugged. "As you wish, mister." He saddled the chestnut.

"Did your sister know Mercer never intended to take you along, kid?" he asked.

"I don't know," replied Gil.

"You're lying," said Lee flatly. "That's why you're here. I told you and that damned fool sister of yours to turn back more than once."

"Don't call my sister a damned fool!" snapped Gil.

"You got a better name for her?" demanded Lee.

Gil led the chestnut to the door and mounted it. He looked down at Lee. "You aim to stand there jawing all night long?" he asked.

"If I want to, sonny," said Lee easily. "Besides, who the hell invited you to come along with me?"

"I did," replied Gil. He leaned forward in the saddle. "And don't start in by telling me how gawddamned tough it's going to be, big man! Just show me the way and forget the bullshit advice!"

Lee grinned as he paid the boy. He looked up at Gil. "Haven't you forgotten something?" he asked. "I'm not paying for that horse and saddle. My 'manhunting' money, as you might call it, doesn't cover that kind of expense." He led the gray and the dun from the stable and then mounted the gray. "Give the kid a tip," he suggested. "That's a good horse he sold you."

Gil kneed his horse from the stable and reined in beside Lee. "I'm riding a little westerly," explained Lee. "We'll cross the Rio Santa Maria and then head into the Sierra del Arco, then south through the foothills toward Namiquipa."

"By that time Lopez will be forty miles away," said Gil dryly.

Lee rode into a side street. "You think Lopez won't cover his retreat without a few of his muchachos left behind?"

"We're not Rurales or Federales," said Gil.

"We're not friends of Lopez either. That sonofabitch Mercer will know I'm still after him, and maybe he figures you'll be after him as well. By this time Lopez's boys will have a detailed description of the both of us. The Galeana garrison was tricked into riding south, supposedly to catch Lopez. It won't be long until they find out that they were tricked. They'll know soon enough that Lopez hit

115

Galeana. So I figure Lopez will ride south just so far and then turn off the road before he runs head-on into the Federales. Now, even if we slipped past Lopez's rear-guard, odds are we might meet up with the Federales. I'll guarantee you that they won't believe I'm not riding with Lopez again. *¡Ley del fuego!* Remember? That's a phrase you love to quote."

"They've got nothing on me," argued Gil.

"The hell they haven't! You're with *me*, aren't you? Or maybe you'd rather go it alone. Eh?"

Gil kept his mouth shut. Lee fished a bottle of brandy out of a saddlebag and held it out to the kid as they rode. "You look like you need this," he suggested. The kid took the bottle and uncorked it. He drank deeply. He slanted his eyes at Lee. "Mother's milk," he said. He grinned.

Some of the years suddenly scaled away. Lee remembered all too well another kid riding boot to boot with him into Mexico with the hands of the Rurales and Federales against them.

They clattered over a wooden bridge that spanned a dry stream. Gil drank again and corked the bottle. He handed it back to Lee. Lee stuffed it back into the saddlebag. He made a cigarette and lighted it, then handed the makings to the kid. They rode up the slopes. Behind them winked the lights of Galeana while a pillar of smoke speckled with fat sparks arose from the eastern side of the plaza.

Lee looked sideways at Gil. "You know what the odds are, don't you, kid?" he asked.

Gil drew in on his cigarette and the glowing of the tip softly lighted his face. "I know," he replied.

They rode steadily to the west through the fading moonlight.

FOURTEEN

THE WIND SHIFTED and brought with it the faint, resinous tang of woodsmoke and the faint murmuring of the voices of many men. Lee Kershaw turned his head sideways and raised his head from his crossed forearms to look at the shadowed face of the kid. "Any bright suggestions?" asked Lee.

Gil slowly shook his head. *"Nada,"* he said.

"That makes two of us," said Lee. He looked down again from the hog-backed ridge from the position he and Gil had taken to overlook the bivouac of the Lopezistas. A fire flared up as wood was carelessly thrown upon it, sending up a swirling pillar of smoke and sparks. Another fire flared up. The soft firelight shone against the peeling, whitewashed walls of the buildings that faced the plaza of the old *poblado*. Grotesque shadows of giant men wearing gigantic steeple-crowned sombreroes passed along the walls as the *revolutionarios* passed between the walls and the many fires that dotted the plaza.

"You've been here before?" Gil asked.

Lee nodded. "Many times," he replied. "This place was abandoned years ago."

"Why?"

Lee shrugged. "Yaqui raids. Plague. A dwindling water supply. Half a dozen revolutions. Lopez is said to have been born here. He took it over a couple of revolutions ago. He knows he's safe here from the Federales."

Gil looked along the ridge and back over his shoulder. "He hasn't any sentries out on this side," he said. "We can move right down into the edge of that *poblado* without being seen."

Lee shifted his chew and spat down the slope. "He doesn't need sentries in these hills," he said.

"Why?"

Lee jerked a thumb back over his shoulder. "Yaquis," he explained. "They like Lopez. They don't like the Federales or the Rurales. No Rurale or Federale could get to within five miles of Lopez while he's in these hills without the Yaquis giving him plenty of warning."

"Yaquis—piss!" Gil said. He shifted his chew and spat down the slope as Lee had done. "They ain't such a much. They let *us* get past them, didn't they?"

Lee nodded. He eyed Gil's shadowy face. "That was because you were with me," he explained.

"What the hell does that mean?"

Lee looked down at the *poblado*. Lopez had at least two hundred men down there, armed to the teeth and aching for a scrap. "You ever figure they *saw* us, sonny?" he asked.

"We didn't see them!"

"Nope. That's exactly what I mean. They knew me from the past."

"You mean to lie there with tobacco juice dribbling down into your whiskers and tell me they actually *saw* us while we came through those hills?"

"Like you said, and I quote: 'Yaquis—piss!' and I might tell you, sonny, that if one of them had wanted to, he could have done just that and you'd never have known it until you suddenly felt wet and warm."

"That's a crock if I ever heard one!" jeered Gil.

Lee yawned. "Go on back alone," he suggested, "and see how far you get."

Gil hesitated. He looked over his shoulder at the bluish black lumps of those brooding hills. An uneasy, crawling feeling came over him and his guts seemed to loosen a little. "Why didn't you tell me?" he asked in a small voice.

Lee grinned crookedly. "I was keeping my own guts cinched up tight as it was to keep from loading my drawers. There wasn't any use in worrying you too, sonny."

"Gives a man the creeps," Gil observed.

"You're getting the general idea," Lee said.

"So, if we do get Leila out of here, we'd still have to get back past the Yaquis, and by that time they'd know you weren't a Lopezista anymore?"

Lee nodded. "Then there are the Federales and the Rurales beyond the Yaquis and then more Yaquis and some Apaches beyond them, and so on and so on. Besides, we'd also have the problem of keeping Mr. Chad Mercer quiet."

Gil slowly turned his head to look at Lee. "You mean you aim to get Chad out of that *poblado*, too?"

"That's why I came here," Lee said.

Gil leaned closer and stabbed a big forefinger toward Lee's expressionless face. "Look, *you*," he warned in a low voice, "we came to get my sister out of here. You, and no one else either, is going to make it any harder to get her out of there. We go in and get her and we forget about Chad Mercer."

"I came all the way down here to get Chad Mercer," said Lee coldly. "Your father practically ran me off of the Querencia to get Mercer for him, sonny. That's what I aim to do. If we can get Leila out of the *poblado* at the same time, *without* my risking losing Mercer, I'll go the route with you."

"God damn you! My Pa ain't paying you to bring back Chad Mercer at the price of leaving my sister down there to be gang-raped by a bunch of stinking greasers! I ought to throw down on you right now!"

Lee casually reached out with a big hand, gathered Gil's neck scarf into a fist, and twisted it tight. He drew Gil's face close to his. "Listen, you juvenile hero," he husked in a low voice. "You go on alone down there and rile up those stinking greasers, as you call them, and they'll have your pants and drawers off in two minutes and they'll castrate you with a knife heated red-hot in one of those fires down there. Or maybe they'll be a little more gentle and just tie you up with your eyelids propped open with crucifixion thorns so you can't miss any of the details while they gang-rape your sister. This is not cowboys and

119

Indians we're playing, mister. We're playing for the highest stakes of all—our lives! Now, you just keep that big mouth of yours tightly shut and do some organized thinking. It was you and that birdbrained sister of yours who got her into this mess. By rights I can walk away from you right now and let the two of you go plumb to hell! You get the idea, sonny? *¿Comprende?*" He shoved Gil back and released his hold on the scarf.

Gil slowly eased the scarf about his neck. He did not take his eyes from Lee. "*Yo comprendo,*" he sullenly admitted.

"Hand me those field glasses, kid," said Lee as though nothing unpleasant had passed between them. He took the glasses and focused them on the plaza, which teemed with the tough vaqueros who rode proudly with Lopez. The firelight reflected dully from weapons and the coin silver bands that encircled the huge sugarloaf sombreroes affected by the Lopezistas. Once Lee thought he recognized the squat and powerful figure of Lopez himself, but he wasn't sure. Then the good German lens picked out the handsome blond-bearded face of Chad Mercer as he talked with a tall Mexican whom Lee recognized as the Captain Santiago who had come into the alleyway and had driven Lee into cover during the Galeana raid. Once he caught the shape of a slim woman he thought might be Leila, but as the firelight flared up against her Lee knew her to be one of those patient, uncomplaining women who followed their men during wars in Mexcio to cook their food and give them their bodies, and who also followed their men right onto the battlefield, sometimes to fight beside them and to bind their wounds, or bury them if need be. There were others of them in the firelighted plaza squatting over the cooking pots or filling their water ollas at the well. Lee wondered idly what they must think of the tall, green-eyed gringa who had involuntarily joined them during the raid on Galeana.

"Can you see her?" asked Gil.

Lee shook his head. "Mercer is down there."

"To hell with Mercer! Where's Leila?"

A priest had walked from the ruins of the church that

dominated the south side of the plaza. Lee grinned to himself. "Padre Antonio," he murmured.

"What's that you say?" asked Gil.

"Nothing. I just saw an old friend, kid."

"When do we go down there?" Gil asked.

Lee rolled over onto his back and looked up at the ice chip stars. "We don't," he said laconically.

"You loco?" demanded Gil.

Lee shook his head. He tapped the side of his temple. "We'd be spotted right off, kid. We've got to play it smart."

"So we run off with our tails between our legs?"

Lee rolled over onto his side to face Gil. "Not exactly, kid," he said. "We're going to try and make a deal."

"What are you talking about?"

"We haven't got a chance of getting your sister and Mercer out of that *poblado*. We'll need help. So we go and get it."

"Here? In Mexico? Are you loco? Who'd help us?"

Lee grinned. "The Federales."

"I had a feeling for some time that the sun out on the Llanos de Carretas had touched your little head. Now I know it!"

Lee looked through the field glasses again. He picked out Chad Mercer and this time he saw Leila, walking beside Mercer toward the ruined church. The faint glowing of candlelight came through the opened double doors of the church. "There's your sister, kid." Lee handed the glasses to Gil. "Going into the church with Mercer." Gil studied his sister and Chad. "That sonofabitch," murmured the kid.

Lee glanced to the east. The first faint traces of moonlight showed beyond the mountains. Gil looked sideways from the glasses. "What's this deal you were talking about?"

"The Federales would almost give up their manhood to get their hands on Lopez, especially after the raid on Galeana. The Federales don't know about this rendezvous here and they couldn't get anywhere near it if they did know about it because of the Yaquis. That's two points in our favor."

"Meaning?"

Lee crawled down the reverse slope and stood up. "I don't know about you, but I'm riding to the Federales to make a deal with them. If I can guide them here by a way they won't be seen by the Yaquis, maybe they'll pay me by turning over Chad Mercer and your sister. With a safe conduct to the border, of course."

"You'd trust those Mex soldiers?"

"You got any better ideas?"

Gil shook his head. He followed Lee down the slope to where they had left the horses. They mounted and rode on rawhide-booted horses through the darkness with Lee leading on the dun. A mile from the *poblado* Gil broke the silence. "What happens if the Federales don't make a deal?" he asked.

Lee shrugged. "*Ley del fuego.*"

They rode another mile. Gil looked sideways at Lee. "You really want Mercer, don't you, Lee?" he asked.

"You're getting the idea," admitted Lee.

"You could just keep on riding north to the border."

Lee shifted his chew and spat. "I came all the way down here for Chad Mercer," he said. He did not speak again as the moon rose and flooded the river valley to the east with clear light.

FIFTEEN

THE BRAZEN VOICE of the bugle gave tongue through the graying darkness just before the coming of the dawn. The call echoed from the dark surrounding hills and then died away. The soft glowing of lamplight showed through the worn canvas of the many tents of the encampment.

Lee Kershaw squatted on his heels and lighted a cigarette. He yawned. "Maybe I better give them time to have their morning coffee," he said. "It just might put them into a better mood."

The bugle sounded again, this time more urgently. More lights blinked on and the faint sound of voices drifted uphill to the two men who waited there. A faint line of dawn light showed along the uneven rim of the eastern mountains. The wind shifted, died out, and then blew harder to chill the two men.

Lee stood up. He unbuckled his gun belt and hung it over his saddlehorn. The graying light showed against the lean planes of his bearded face. "What happens if they don't buy your story?" asked Gil. Lee drew in on the cigarette and the glowing of the tip lighted his blue eyes. "Then, it's all up to you, isn't it, kid?" he asked.

"Would they believe me?" asked Gil.

Lee shrugged. "They have a saying, *after* they shoot the innocent by mistake," he said.

"Such as?"

"God will sort the souls."

Gil shrugged in turn as he lighted a cigarette. "They got nothing on me," he said.

"The Romans had nothing on Jesus," countered Lee.

"You have a neat way of putting things," said Gil.

"You'll have to make your own decision, kid, if anything happens to me down there. You can either go down and talk to the Federales or go back to the *poblado* and make a hero out of yourself by trying it single-handed. In that case, the Mexes might even write a *canción* about you—you know, a ballad about the heroic young gringo who tried to save his sister from the hands of the Lopezistas and who died in the attempt. Or you can still make the border. You've got three good horses. Ride at night. Hide out by day. Don't camp by the waterholes. Make no fires and watch for rising dust."

Gil inspected his cigarette as though he had never seen one quite like it before. "Maybe I ought to go down there with you," he suggested.

Lee shook his head. "It's my job, kid." He took a brandy bottle from a saddlebag and pulled out the cork with his

123

teeth. He offered the bottle first to the kid. Gil shook his head. Lee upended the bottle and drank deeply. He lowered it, wiped his mouth, shook the bottle a little, upended it again, and drained it. He rammed in the cork and hurled the empty soldier high into the air over a clump of ocotillo.

"Brandy is the drink for heroes," said Gil.

Lee nodded. "You're getting the idea, kid." His eyes were a little bright. He quickly rolled a quirly and placed it between his lips. He fanned a match against the fabric of his levis and lighted the cigarette. He slanted his sombrero rakishly to one side and then looked at the eastern sky. The sun was just below the serrated edge of the rim of mountains. *"Es el día!"* he exclaimed. He set off down the slope in long, swinging strides.

"Vaya con Dios!" Gil called out.

Lee waved a hand. He did not look back.

Gil uncased the field glasses and blew on the lens and then slowly polished them with his scarf. He led the three horses into a hollow and picketed them, but he did not unsaddle the chestnut and the gray. He walked back to where he could look down on the encampment and sat down on the ground with his back against a boulder. He could see Lee's rangy figure moving down the brush-stippled slope toward the first sentry post. The gray light of dawn filled the great valley. Here and there a vagrant tumbleweed rolled before the cold wind. The sun tipped the mountains. Bugles and drums sounded down on the parade ground between the rows of bell tents. The flag of Mexico moved jerkily up a tall, warped flagpole and then snapped out in the strong morning breeze as the bugles and drums saluted it.

Lee halted a hundred yards from the sentry. Lee dropped his cigarette and slowly ground out the butt beneath a boot sole. He rested his hands atop his sombrero and walked easily toward the sentry. The sentry whirled and thrust forward his long rolling-block rifle. "Halt! Who goes there?" he challenged.

Lee promptly halted. "Friend!" he called out.

"Advance one to be recognized!" snapped the sentry.

Lee looked behind him. He was all alone. He looked back at the sentry as he approached the post. "Call the Corporal of the Guard," Lee suggested.

"Corporal of the Guard! Post Number One!" yelled out the sentry.

A burly soldier burst from a tent near the post and trotted up to the post. His eyes narrowed as he saw Lee. "You!" he said. Lee nodded easily. "The colonel will want to see you," said the noncom. He grinned, revealing strong white teeth. "Follow me, señor."

Lee followed the corporal across the windy parade ground, followed by the eyes of the shako-hatted Regulars of the Sixth Mounted Infantry. Lee knew of them as a tough, hardcased outfit that had served along the border since Benito Juarez had become *presidente* of Mexico and they had less use for a blue-eyed gringo mercenary who fought with Lopez than they had for the native breed of Lopezista.

"Who is colonel now?" asked Lee of the corporal.

The corporal looked slantways at Lee. "Diaz," he replied.

"Sebastiano Diaz?" asked Lee with an uncomfortable feeling.

"Who else?" The corporal grinned. "I think he will well remember you, hombre."

"I *know* he will," murmured Lee.

The corporal pointed to a large double-wall tent that stood alone. He watched Lee curiously as Lee pulled aside the tent flap and bent his head to enter the tent. He looked up into the hard agate eyes of Colonel Sebastiano Diaz. "Good morning, my colonel," said Lee.

Diaz studied Lee. "Cut the bullshit, as you Yanquis say, Kershaw. Are you without reason or mind to come here?"

Lee smiled. "I have a deal, Colonel," he suggested.

"I do not deal with Yanqui mercenaries!" snapped Diaz.

"You might deal with this one," said Lee quietly. "You want Lopez, don't you?"

"Of course I do! Do you know where he is?"

"I do," replied Lee.

Diaz leaned forward. "Good! Then I can wring that information out of you without making a *deal,* as you call it."

Lee nodded. "Agreed. But you know as well as I do that even if I tell you where Lopez and his men are, that's no guarantee that you can get to him without me showing you the way past the Yanquis."

Diaz leaned back and toyed with a letter opener shaped like a miniature saber. "Were you at Galeana with Lopez?"

"I was there," admitted Lee. "I was not *with* him."

"*Why* were you there?" demanded Diaz.

"On business," replied Lee. "I was looking for a man."

"Who?"

"The man known as Chad Mercer," answered Lee.

Diaz showed no surprise. "I know he is again riding with Lopez. It is said there is a green-eyed *gringa* with him. Is she, perhaps, planning to be his camp follower?" Diaz smiled a little.

"She is with him," admitted Lee. "She is not his camp follower. If you agree to let me lead you to Lopez, I want Mercer and the green-eyed gringa in return."

Diaz wiped his mustache both ways. He studied Lee closely. "I take it that you want to save your old compañero from the firing squad. Is that correct?"

"Yes. *Your* firing squad, that is."

"I do not understand."

Lee took the plunge. "May I remove my left boot?" he asked.

Diaz shrugged. "You always were rather informal. Go ahead if it makes you more comfortable. I hope, however, that you have changed your socks within the last month."

"Very funny," said Lee dryly. He sat down and yanked off his left boot. He reached over and took the letter opener from Diaz and then slit the boot lining. He took out the warrant for the arrest of Chad Mercer and placed it on the desk in front of the officer. Diaz wrinkled his fine aquiline nose as he read the warrant. Lee slit the lining of the right boot and withdrew his deputy star. He placed it beside the warrant. Diaz fingered the star. He looked up at Lee. "You are hunting down your best friend to bring him back to New Mexico for possible execution?" he asked. "Why?"

"That's my job," replied Lee.

"Manhunter," said Diaz in a tone tinged with contempt.

Lee nodded. "It's a living."

"Evidently it must pay you more than riding with Lopez."

"Lopez still owes me money from the last time," said Lee.

Diaz shook his head. "I find all this difficult to understand."

Lee leaned forward. "Forget that," he suggested. "You want Lopez. I want Mercer. I can get you Lopez. If I put Lopez in your hands, I want you to give me the man Mercer and the green-eyed gringa with him. In addition, I want twenty-four hours start for the border."

Diaz leaned back. "I could have you shot right now," he said thoughtfully. "I *should* have you shot right now," he corrected himself.

Lee shook his head. "Aren't you long overdue for that brigadier-generalship? The one you should have had before Lopez defeated you at El Corralitos?"

"I seem to remember you being there," said Diaz coldly.

Lee replaced the warrant and the star in his boots. He felt for his tobacco canteen and began to fashion a cigarette, but his eyes never left Diaz. The bugle sounded. The sound of tramping feet came from the parade ground. A mule brayed from a corral. Galloping hoofs sounded beyond the encampment. The sun was beginning to warm the tent canvas.

Diaz moved. "Would you like coffee?" he asked.

A surge of relief flowed through Lee, but he did not expose his feelings. A cold worm of sweat worked out of each armpit and trickled icily down his sides. "*Gracias,*" he mumured.

"*Por nada.* You have a horse?"

"Three," replied Lee.

Diaz raised his eyebrows. "So many?" he asked in surprise.

"There is a companion waiting for me up in the hills," explained Lee.

"And he too is in on this 'deal'?"

127

"That is so," replied Lee. He lighted his cigarette. He blew a smoke ring. "He is the brother of the green-eyed gringa."

Diaz walked to the tent flap and thrust out his head. "Coffee!" he called out. He came back to his desk and sat down. "Somewhere there is a good story?" he suggested.

"Someday I'll tell it to you over a glass of brandy," replied Lee.

Diaz nodded. An orderly came into the tent with coffee and served the two men then left the tent. Diaz sipped at the strong brew. "When do we leave?" he asked.

"At dusk. Send your men out in small details of ten or a dozen men. Establish a rendezvous near the break in the hills fifteen miles southwest of here. We must get into those hills before the rising of the moon. There is a place where we can hide until the moon dies. We can move into position with an hour to spare before the dawn."

"That is good," said Diaz. He refilled the coffee cups. "You might have made a good soldier," he suggested.

"Perhaps I was, with Lopez," Lee replied. "I didn't like the hours and the pay."

"Did you ever think that reward money, such as you plan to collect for delivering the man Mercer to your authorities, is like Judas money?"

"Never," replied Lee. Their eyes seemed to lock across the short space between them and it was Diaz who first looked away.

"Bring in your friend and your horses," said Diaz. "Feed and water them. Courtesy of the Republic of Mexico."

"Gracias," said Lee as he stood up.

"Por nada," replied the officer with a casual wave of a hand. He waited until Lee left the tent and then he walked to the door flap and pulled it aside. He watched the tall gringo stride right across the center of the sunlighted parade ground toward the camp entry. Diaz looked down at his colonel's insignia. He had worn them for a long time. Already it almost seemed as though he saw the single star of a brigadier-general there instead.

SIXTEEN

THE SIXTH MOUNTED INFANTRY moved into position in the thick and windless darkness before the coming of the false dawn. Below their position was the old *poblado* cupped in a hollow of the dark hills and enveloped in silence. Now and then a red eye of fire peeped out from the thick ashes of a dying fire. The smoke rose straight upward in the windless air. As the soldiers moved into position leather squeaked and now and then a boot struck against a stone or metal clinked against metal to be echoed by the cursing of the low-voiced noncoms. The sound could hardly have been heard down at the bivouac of the Lopezistas.

Colonel Diaz squatted beside Lee Kershaw and looked down at the quiet *poblado*. "How many men does he have?" he asked.

Lee shrugged. "Two hundred—perhaps another fifty or so."

"Is that all? Are you sure?"

Lee looked sideways at the officer. He shifted his chew and spat down the slope. He wiped his mouth with the back of a hand. "Lopez has a magic," said Lee. "He can make a dozen men act like a score or more."

"There must be more than two hundred of them," insisted Diaz.

Gil spoke up. "There are many women down there."

Lee shifted his weight a little. "Maybe they make Lopez look like an army, Colonel."

"What happens to them?" Gil asked.

Diaz glanced at him. "The same as the men," he said.

"That isn't right," said Gil.

Lee looked at the kid. "Some of them fight harder and more vicious than the men, kid—like Apache and Yaqui squaws. I've seen them get at the enemy wounded with their knives."

Gil shook his head. "It's not right," he insisted. "This isn't civilized warfare."

"Who claimed it was?" asked Lee.

Diaz nodded. "The boy has not been blooded in this type of guerrilla fighting, Kershaw."

"He will be by the time the sun rises," promised Lee.

Gil walked away into the darkness.

"He has no stomach for this," said Diaz.

"He's learning," said Lee. He spat again. "You can move out the first company now, Colonel. Have them follow that deep arroyo west of the *poblado* and take up position there. They will have a clear field of fire right over the tops of those fallen ruins. I suggest you place another company east of the *poblado* but out of the line of fire of those in the arroyo. Those damned rolling-block Remingtons carry too far. Once the fire opens up from the arroyo, Lopez and his boys will try for the east and the lower ground. That's when the company there can catch them on the run from the flank."

"What about the north?" asked Diaz.

"Forget it," replied Lee. "It's just a mite too far for the Lopezistas to reach the safety of the hills. Those Remingtons can reach out and knock them down like tenpins if they try to get up those steep slopes. Besides, the horses are corraled to the east, just beyond the plaza. If the Lopezistas try for their horses, you've got a mounted company there to clean up on them."

Diaz looked back over his shoulder. A horse whinnied softly in the darkness. "And my two remaining mounted companies charge down this slope once Lopez breaks for his horses and strike him from the rear?"

"You're learning, Colonel," said Lee dryly.

"I said before that you should have been a soldier."

"Lopez always thought so too, but, like I said before: I don't like the hours and the pay, Colonel."

Lee squatted there in the darkness with his long arms

hanging over his knees, looking down into the dark *poblado* as he felt, rather than heard, the stealthy movements of soldiers and horses moving into position. There was no sign yet of the false dawn in the eastern sky. Diaz came softly through the brush with his spurs chiming faintly. He unholstered his revolver and spun the cylinder. The dry, metallic whirring sounded clearly in the quietness. "You move in with me, Kershaw?" the colonel asked.

Lee nodded. "I hope to God your men all know me and the kid," he said.

Diaz shrugged. "How can they miss?" he asked.

Lee looked up at him and grinned. "That's a two-edged question, my colonel."

"I can't be responsible for accidents to your two people down there in the *poblado*, Kershaw."

Lee's face hardened. He got slowly to his feet. "The hell you can't!" he snapped.

Diaz' face was granite hard. "Don't talk that way to me again, mister. Never!"

"We made a deal! I kept my part of the bargain!"

Diaz nodded curtly. "I will keep that deal. You have my word as an officer and a gentleman."

Lee checked his Colt and his rifle. Gil came up behind him. "You still got some of that brandy?" he asked. Lee handed him the flask. He drank deep and then again. He raised the bottle for the third time, but a hard hand clamped on his wrist. "That's enough for now," said Lee.

"You my nursey maid now?" demanded Gil.

Lee drank and then lowered the flask. "Someone has to be," he replied. He replaced the flask inside his coat. He looked sideways at Diaz. The dawn wind was beginning to whisper up the slopes. The faintest pewter tinge showed in the eastern sky. Diaz beckoned to his orderly. The orderly led up the colonel's fine black horse. Diaz mounted, then drew his saber from its scabbard with a slithering of steel. Over a hundred other sabers followed suit. The bugler single-footed his horse up and reined it in just behind the colonel.

The moment hung in the balance as though time had

stopped for a quick breather before plunging onward to meet the dawn. The dawn light grew infinitesimally. Diaz stood up in his stirrups and looked down at the *poblado*. Someone moved down in the plaza, kicking a dying fire into life. Here and there in clumps and individual mounds the blankets moved a little as men stirred sleepily before rising. A burro brayed hoarsely from the corral. Diaz looked to the northwest, toward the shadowed arroyo. He raised his pistol and cocked it. The mounted men moved restlessly in their saddles. Diaz tightened his pistol hand. The pistol cracked flatly and the echo slammed back and forth between the dark hills and before it died away, it was drowned out by a tearing volley that leaped from the dark lip of the arroyo with stabbing viper tongues of orange-red flames.

Men screamed and yelled as the heavy soft lead slugs tore into them. Some Lopezistas died before they could awaken. The soldiers fired as fast as they could reload, hardly bothering to take aim as a scythe of bullets swept right over the tumbled ruins into the plaza, tumbling more men atop those who had already fallen. A fire flared up, licking hungrily at the blankets of a dead Lopezista.

Diaz looked back over his shoulder. "Play the Charge," he commanded the bugler. The bugler lipped into the strident summons. The firing from the arroyo ceased as abruptly as it had begun. Diaz raised his saber. *"Degüello!"* he shrieked at the bugler.

"What's that, Lee?" Gil yelled as he mounted.

"No Quarter!" flung out Lee as he spurred down the slope after Diaz. The chilling, dreadful notes of the no-quarter bugle call of Old Spain seemed to race down the slope ahead of the charging Mexicans.

The Lopezistas, those that were not dead, dying, or too seriously wounded to run, broke in panic as they heard the *degüello* and ran for the corrals on the lower ground to the east of the *poblado*. The mounted charge struck them in the right flank as they ran. Sabers rose and fell and men were scattered into the side streets cut off from their horses. Those that did reach the corral were caught in the flame-sheeted vollies from the dismounted company south of the corrals. Those few that reached the horses and rode down the slight eastern slope were met by pistol shots and flailing sabers from the mounted company Lee had advised Diaz to post there. Lopezistas, stung from behind by the fire from the arroyo, struck in the flank by Diaz's charge, cut off from the corral by the firing of the dismounted company, had swung panic-stricken to the north to try to reach the steep slope of the hills just north of the *poblado*. The soldiers in the arroyo raised their sights and fired into the backs of the stampeded *revolutionarios,* driving them face forward to the hard ground or catching them on the slopes as they clawed desperately for handholds and footholds on the sterile surface. Not one man reached the crest.

A pall of acrid powdersmoke rose heavily to meet the swiftly growing dawn light. Lee rounded the side of the church and saw the familiar squat, broad-shouldered figure of Lopez, weighted down with crisscross cartridge belts, running with his awkward horseman's gait toward the corrals. Diaz passed Lee like a riding fury, closing in behind Lopez like a Cossack at a pogrom, to slash down with his razor-edged saber right through the heavy felt sombrero, taking off the left ear in the process. Lopez shrieked like a wounded mare. The second slash took off his right ear with neat precision. He whirled to throw up his arms in defense, but the saber swept down with terrible force and sheared off his forehead skin, his nose and lips. He staggered sideways, a faceless, bleeding wreck from which shone two terrible eyes, shrieking through a lipless mouth.

"For the love of God, Colonel!" screamed Gil.

Lee looked sideways at Gil as Lee reined in his dun. "You never heard of what Lopez and his merry boys did to Diaz's younger brother when they captured him wounded after El Corralitos!" he yelled. "It would have made a Yaqui sick to his guts!"

Gil freed his rifle from its sheath and swept it upward, working the lever as he did so. He aimed at the faceless *revolutionario* who was trying to escape the flailing, pitiless saber of Colonel Diaz. Gil fired. Lopez took a slug right through the heart and fell like an ox in the slaughterhouse. Diaz whirled and spurred toward Gil with upraised bloody saber. Lee rode in between them. "You had your damned vengeance, Diaz!" he yelled. "Now finish the slaughter!" Diaz turned as though in a dream and rode off after his yelling men.

A woman screamed in a side street. Gil turned his horse toward her. A soldier was thrusting at Leila Luscombe with a bloody saber. Gil fired and the bullet struck the soldier between the shoulder blades. Gil leaped his horse over the body. Lee looked back over his shoulder. No one but Lee and Leila had likely seen Gil kill the soldier. "Where's Mercer?" yelled Lee to Leila.

A man broke from the doorway of an adobe and legged it up the street away from the plaza. The dun leaped into racing speed. Lee leaned from the saddle and laid the barrel of his Colt right alongside Chad's skull over the left ear. Chad went rump over head into the filthy gutter and lay still. Lee swung down, hooked a boot under Chad, flipped him over on his back and had the cuffs on him in a matter of seconds. He picked him up and threw the limp form over the saddle on the dun. "Come on!" he yelled at the two Luscombes.

"Go get the gray, kid!" Lee ordered as he led the dun into the thick brush that had encroached on the end of the street. He dumped Mercer from the saddle into the cruel thorn-tipped brush and then mounted the dun. He crashed through the brush to grab at the reins of a riderless infantryman's horse. He led the bay horse back to Leila. "Mount!" he snapped at her.

Her eyes were wide in her pale face. "They're killing them all," she said in a strange voice.

"You've got the idea, sister," he said coldly.

Gil rode up to the brush leading Lee's gray and a supply mule that was loaded with full kyacks. The brand of the Republic of Mexico showed on the mule's dusty flank. "Figured we might need rations," Gil said, grinning.

"Sometimes you actually use that hard head of yours," Lee said.

"Which way do we ride?" he asked.

"Due north," Lee answered as he hoisted Mercer over the bare back of the gray. Lee swiftly tied Mercer's hands and feet together under the belly of the gray.

"That's Yaqui territory," said Gil.

Lee mounted the dun and took the reins of the gray. "They'll be five miles from those hills by now and moving fast into the mountains. They won't be out of there before next spring. They saw what happened to Lopez and they don't want any of *that*! We can ride all day today."

They skirted the *poblado*. Scattered shots still sounded and then sudden fusillades broke forth like the ripping of heavy canvas. As the sun arose, the flies began to wing steadily into the blood-soaked plaza of the *poblado*. It was fiesta time for them.

SEVENTEEN

THE GRAY HORSE had gone down for the final count ten miles back. Now it was the bay that Chad Mercer was now riding that stumbled and went down. Chad just managed to kick free from the stirrups and get free from the saddle. He thrust his handcuffed hands out in front of him. "Damn you, Kershaw!" he snarled. "I could have busted my neck! Take off these damned cuffs!"

Lee reined in the dun and looked back at Mercer through the fading dusk light. "You can walk with your hands cuffed," he said.

Gil swung down from the pack mule and looked at its lathered jaws. He looked at Lee. "We keep on this way," he said, "and we won't have a mount left by midnight. They need water worse than we do, Lee."

"When the sun comes up, Kershaw might get it through

his thick head that there isn't a waterhole for thirty miles," said Chad.

"We've got to rest these animals," Gil said.

Lee looked back through the gathering dusk light. A pinpoint of light flicked on and then out. "Not with the Federales not more than five miles behind us," he said.

"Diaz gave you twenty-four hours," reminded Gil.

"And you believed him," said Lee.

"He made a deal! He's an officer and a gentleman!" snapped Gil.

Lee slid from the saddle. "You're a trusting soul, kid."

Leila dismounted from Gil's chestnut. "Deal?" she asked. "What kind of a deal?"

Lee looked behind her and shook his head at Gil.

"Gil?" asked Leila sharply.

"We couldn't get you and Chad out of that *poblado*," replied Gil. "Not just the two of us. Lee went to Diaz's encampment and made a deal. Lee was to lead Diaz around the Yaquis to come in from the south with a surprise attack. In return Diaz agreed we could have you and Chad, with a twenty-four-hour safe conduct to the border."

"You can forget about *that* part of the deal," Lee said dryly.

Leila looked quickly at Lee. "You turned Diaz and his killers loose on Lopez and his men and their women, knowing what Diaz would do?" she demanded.

Lee shrugged. "It was really only a matter of time," he replied. "Lopez used up all his luck on that Galeana raid. Diaz would have gotten him eventually."

"But they slaughtered those people!" cried Leila.

"I didn't know Diaz planned *degüello*. Not until he ordered the bugle call," Lee explained.

"You're lying! You'd do anything to get your man, wouldn't you?"

Lee leaned against his dun. "We got *you* out of there, didn't we?" he asked.

"I was all right," she said.

Lee shook his head. "How long do you think Lopez would have let Chad Mercer keep you as his personal

136

woman in that camp? In a week every one of his officers would have had you, after Lopez, of course, and in a month you would have been out on the plaza with the women, sleeping with any man who'd hand you a crust of bread and a pot of beans."

"That's not so!" she cried.

Chad yawned. He worked his shoulders to loosen them up. "Tell him, Leila," he suggested.

"We were married at the *poblado*," she said.

Gil's head snapped around. "You didn't tell me," he said.

Lee eyed her. This was something new.

"Legally?" Gil asked.

She nodded. "By General Lopez's priest," she replied.

Lee looked past her at Chad Mercer. A faint smile was on Mercer's face. "Padre Antonio?" asked Lee.

"Yes," said Leila. "So, you see, we are man and wife. Even General Lopez would have respected that."

Lee looked to the south. Once again he picked up that faint pinpoint of light. All the time the four of them were standing there discussing the marital status of Leila and Chad, the Federales were closing in on them. Lee picked up the dun's reins. "Come on," he ordered. "We're at least fifteen miles from the border." He led the dun on along the faint trail and then slanted off toward the northwest.

"Where the hell do you think you're going?" demanded Chad.

"Tanques Perdido," replied Lee.

"Lost Tanks? Are you loco? There's no water there at this time of the year!"

"We'll take that chance," said Lee.

"You're not even sure where they are!"

"We'll take that chance, too."

"Damn you to hell! Not with *our* lives, you don't!"

Lee halted and turned. "You want to wait here for the Federales, mister? You know what you'll get. *Ley del fuego!*"

"I'll take that chance!" snapped Chad.

Lee shook his head. "The choice isn't yours. I've got a deal to deliver you, packaged, sealed, and stamped, to

Sheriff Luscombe. I'm making the decisions here, mister. Get moving! ¡*Andale!*"

Chad looked back over his shoulder. "You're not even sure it's them," he said.

"Does it make any difference *who* it is? Maybe it's some of the Lopezistas. It won't make any difference to them that you once rode with Lopez. It might be Yaquis or Apaches. Maybe you'd like to wait here alone and find out?"

There was no answer from Chad. Lee walked on. Gil drew up abreast of Lee, leading the worn-out pack mule. "What about those tanks, Lee?" he asked quietly. He glanced back toward his sister, who was now walking beside Chad, leading the chestnut. "Is what Chad said true?" added Gil.

"¿*Quién sabe?*" Lee said. He took out his tobacco plug and bit off a chew. He offered the plug to the kid. "Keeps down the dryness, kid," he said.

Gil shook his head. "What's the odds, Lee?" he asked.

Lee shrugged. "All I know is that we can't stand here."

"That's Apache country, isn't it?"

"The whole damned country around here is," replied Lee.

They walked on for ten minutes. Gil looked back. "You really think they're married?" he asked.

Lee shifted his chew and spat forcefully. "In a way," he answered. He wiped his mouth with the back of a hand.

"What the hell does that mean? They're either married or they ain't!"

"Nothing, kid. Forget it."

"No! You've got to tell me!"

Lee glanced over his shoulder. "They were married by a priest. Isn't that enough?"

"I saw the look on your face when she told us."

"You've got a suspicious mind, kid."

Gil studied Lee's face. "Lee," he asked quietly. "Was that a *real* priest?"

"¿*Quién sabe?*"

"You know, don't you?" persisted Gil.

Lee glanced at him. "So do you," he said.

"God damn him to hell!"

Lee thumbed the kid's shoulder with a jabbing motion. "Don't tell her," he warned.

Gil opened and closed his mouth. He looked at Lee and then back at his sister and Chad. "All right," he agreed. "But one of these days me and Mr. Mercer are going to have a nice long, quiet talk."

"You might not beat the hangrope, kid," suggested Lee. "Do you believe Frank was murdered by Chad?"

"No," replied the kid.

"You're not even sure about that, are you?"

"You ask too many damned fool questions!"

Lee shrugged. "Let's leave it at that, then," he said. "Only your father seemed damned sure of his evidence against Chad."

The low hills began to rise up on either side of them as they passed beyond the lower ground of the Llanos de Carretas. Now and then a hoof struck a stone to sound like a cracked bell. There was a brooding quality in the thick darkness of the hills. The heat still hung heavily in the shallow canyons, not yet dispelled by the cooler night air. Now and then Gil Luscombe would glance furtively sideways at the tall, gaunt man who walked beside him on and on through the hot, clinging darkness, never losing a full stride and only breaking the rhythmn of his movement now and then to turn his head sideways to spit out tobacco juice.

The moon arose and flooded its light across the Llanos de Carretas. Lee held up a hand for a halt. He reached inside his nearest saddlebag and withdrew a brandy bottle. Lee offered the bottle to Gil, but Gil shook his head. Lee upended the bottle and drank deeply.

"Save one for me," suggested Chad Mercer.

Lee lowered the bottle, glanced at Chad, then upended the bottle. He lowered it and then hurled it high in among the broken rocks that cascaded down the canyon side.

"*Gracias*," said Chad.

"*Por nada*," replied Lee.

"Look!" cried Gil. He pointed back along the canyon and across the rough ground they had crossed when they had left the Llanos de Carretas. Something dark was moving to the north along the trail that Lee had left hours back.

"Federales, most likely," said Lee.

"I hope they find water north of here," said Gil. He grinned.

"They will," said Lee.

Gil's head jerked toward Lee. "What the hell do you mean?" he demanded.

Lee picked up the dun's reins. "There's a watering place not five miles ahead of them from where they are now. You'll remember it—the abandoned *poblado*."

"Jesus! Why didn't *we* go there?"

"Simple," replied Lee. "They *expected* us to go there. Odds are that Diaz must have telegraphed ahead to the garrison far to the east of the abandoned *poblado* and had them send out a detail west toward the *poblado*. They might even be there now, still waiting for us." Lee walked on, leading the tired dun.

"Lost Tanks!" said Chad. "Mother of God! He's leading us to our deaths!"

Gil looked up the canyon toward the broad, sweat-soaked back of Lee Kershaw. "Go on back, Chad," suggested Gil. "It'll save the county the expense of a trial and a hanging." Gil walked on after Lee, leading the pack mule.

Leila looked up into Chad's bearded face. "We two can go back," she suggested. "Will the Federales really harm us?"

He looked down at her. "No. Not *you*! But what about *me?* They won't waste any time on me. They've got their orders from Diaz."

"But we'd at least be sure of water if we went back," suggested Leila. "We can't go on much longer like this, Chad."

"Christamighty! Go on back, then! Think of yourself, Leila! Forget about me! I'm only your husband!"

She looked up the slopes toward Lee and Gil. "You can make a break for it now," she suggested.

"With these bracelets on and with a horse that's ready to drop? Where could I go? I can't go back there with the

Federales sitting at the only water, just waiting for me! Use your goddamned head, woman!"

For a moment she studied his hard and bitter face and then she nodded. "I intend to use my goddamned head, Chad," she said quietly. She picked up the reins of the chestnut and led it up the sloping floor of the canyon and she did not look back.

Chad looked down toward the plains. He held up his cuffed hands and tugged viciously at them until the blood ran down his wrists. "Damn him!" he spat out. "Oh, God-damn him!" He started up the slope after Leila.

EIGHTEEN

THE LAST OF THE moonlight still touched the hills and mountains to the west. An uncertain wind shifted back and forth through the wide canyon that trended north into higher land. Gil Luscombe stood up and peered down into the canyon. "There's no one there," he said.

Lee turned his head. "Shut up and sit down," he ordered. "Your voice can be heard half a mile up the canyon with this wind blowing."

Gil squatted beside Lee. "We've been here an hour," he said hoarsely. "How do you know there are Apaches down there?"

"We might be here all night," said Lee. He shifted his chew. "I don't have to see them, kid. I feel 'em!"

"Gil is right," said Chad Mercer from the darkness under a huge overhanging ledge. "There's no one down there."

"Helluva lot you know," observed Lee.

"You think you're so gawddamned smart!" sneered Chad.

"Go on down there, hombre," suggested Lee. He took out the key to the handcuffs. "Turn him loose, kid. Let the *big* man go down there and see if there's no one at the tanks."

Gil couldn't help but grin a little. "How about it, Chad?" he asked over his shoulder.

"You're as bad as he is," growled Chad.

The chestnut had dropped three miles back. Now it was the mule that was showing bad sign. He was restless, shifting back and forth, raising his head and breathing hard, making thirsty noises. Lee unsheathed his knife and handed it to the kid. "Get rid of him," he ordered.

"We'll need him," protested Gil.

Lee shook his head. "He won't keep his big mouth shut. He knows there's water down there and he'll let the whole damned canyon know about it any minute now."

Gil stood up. He looked uncertainly down at Lee.

Lee looked up. "What's the matter? Can't you kill him quietly?"

"Sure."

"Then do it! Lead him back down the hill. Wait until the wind blows toward you and then let him have it. *¡Andale!*"

Gil nodded. He walked down the dark slope.

"What about the packs?" asked Chad.

"What about the packs?" mimicked Lee.

"We haven't eaten all day."

"Go cut yourself a mule steak," suggested Lee.

"You bastard!"

"*Gracias*," murmured Lee. He went bellyflat and worked his way down the harsh slope, mentally cursing the wait-a-bit thorns that ripped at his flesh and clothing. The sour odor of sweat clung about him. He wondered if the Apaches down at the tanks might be able to smell him when the wind blew their way.

Lee lay still as the moon waned and died. He couldn't see or hear anyone down at those tanks, but something had warned him—a subtle sixth sense that had been honed by years of living in hostile country. Yet it wasn't like Apaches or Yaquis to stop for water and then camp beside the water. That was a fool white man's way of doing things.

A stone clicked on the slope above Lee. Then Gil bellied alongside Lee and handed him the knife. "Never made a sound," he reported in a whisper. Lee sheathed the still-warm knife. "That's more than I can say for you coming down that slope," he hissed.

Gil looked down the slope. "You still think there's someone down there?" he asked.

"Who knows? It's not like Apaches or Yaquis to camp near water. They hate being surprised worse than anything. They usually water up, then head for the nearest heights away from the water. It might not be Apaches at that, but there's *somebody* down there!"

"*We're* on the heights," whispered the kid. "We don't seem to have any company."

Lee nodded. "That's what bothers me."

Gil rested his chin on his crossed forearms. "We've got to get that water," he said.

Lee quickly raised his head. The wind had shifted. It had raked itself across a bed of ashes down near the tanks. Red ember eyes suddenly appeared through the ashes like brilliant rubies displayed on black velvet. A figure walked past the fire and was gone as swiftly and mysteriously as it had appeared.

"You were dead right," Gil whispered to Lee.

Lee uncased his field glasses and focused them on the area of the tanks. As the vagrant wind played carelessly with the fire Lee could just make out several blanketed forms on the ground. A horse whinnied softly from the thick darkness north beyond the tanks and was echoed by another horse. Lee lowered the glasses. He spat sideways. "Damned sure of themselves," he murmured. "We'll need some of those horses."

"You aim to steal horses from *them?*" The kid was incredulous. "You'll never get away with it."

Lee looked sideways. "You got the guts to go down there with me and take 'em?" he whispered.

Gil hesitated. "Have we got any choice?" he asked at last.

Lee shook his head.

"I'll go," whispered Gil.

"There's at least six of them down there and likely more," the dry voice whispered just behind them. "You'll need me too, Lee."

Gil jerked his head over his shoulder, but Lee did not move. "I don't trust you, Mercer," Lee said.

"Like the kid figured, you haven't got any choice," replied Chad.

Lee took out the handcuff key and handed it to the kid. "Turn him loose," he whispered.

"I'll need a gun," said Chad.

Lee nodded. "Stay here," he said. He worked his way silently up the slope and over the rim past the overhanging ledge where Leila sat alone. Lee went to his dun and felt within a saddlebag for a short-barreled Colt he sometimes carried beneath his coat in a halfbreed holster. He withdrew his rifle from its scabbard and walked back to her. He handed her the stingy Colt. "We're going down," he said softly. "It'll take all three of us. If we don't make it, you'll have to stick it out up here until they leave the waterhole. When they leave, go down and get your water, then ride due north through the hills. Ride by night and stay hidden by day. Somewhere across the border you should pick up the lights of a ranch."

She looked up at his shadowed face. "And don't let them take me alive," she added. "You forgot to tell me that."

He nodded and then was gone through the darkness without a sound. She shivered a little. He moved through the night like a ghost.

Lee worked his way down the slope. He handed the rifle to Gil. "Give Chad your Colt," he whispered. "Leave your hat and spurs here." Chad took the Colt from Gil and checked it to make sure it was loaded. He looked at Lee. "We go in first?" he whispered.

"Keno," said Lee. "Kid, you lay back. I'll show you where to take your position. If they get past us, it'll be up to you to stop them." He looked up the slope to where Leila was hidden—his meaning was plain enough.

Lee pointed down the slope. "¡*Andale!*" he said. He went down the slope without making a sound and was followed by Chad, who moved as silently and as swiftly as Lee. Gil followed Chad, sweating coldly in the effort to keep from making a sound.

The wind was playing about, rising and falling, shifting uncertainly back and forth. The fire flared up now and then and the wind carried the bittersweet smell of the dying embers up the hill. Nothing moved near the tanks except the thin flickering of little flames that rose and fell from the thick bed of ashes to paint in soft colors the semicircle of huge boulders that surrounded the rock tanks on all sides except the north.

Lee looked back at the kid. He pointed out a position where Gil could fire down on both sides of the boulders to stop any charge the Apaches might make if they got past Chad and Lee. Lee faded into the darkness near the southern base of the boulders.

A man moved softly through the darkness. He raised his head and looked about when he was a good fifty feet from the boulders. He fumbled with the front of his breechclout and spread out his legs. A knife fanged out of the darkness and hooked itself about the buck's corded throat. The Apache never made a sound as he fell forward into his own puddle.

Lee snaked through the darkness on his belly with Chad just behind him. Something moved in the thick shadow of a boulder. A man stepped out into better light, holding a rifle in his hands. He was looking toward the place where Lee had knifed the first Apache. Chad slid into the shadow of the boulders and nodded to Lee. Lee bellied along the ground, then tossed a pebble far behind him. The sentry catfooted through the dimness, looking beyond where Lee lay on the ground. A hooked muscular forearm came around the sentry's throat from behind him. Chad bent backward, lifting the sentry from the ground. The buck never made a sound. His moccasined heels drummed briefly on the hard earth. Lee closed in with his knife, driving it hard upward beneath the rib cage to reach the heart. Lee caught the falling rifle as Chad eased the dead buck to the ground. Chad grinned. He raised two fingers, then vanished soundlessly into the darkness.

Lee stepped across the corpse and flattened himself against a huge boulder. Nothing moved except his rising and falling chest and his probing eyes. Someone coughed near the fire. The fire was almost completely out. The wind stirred the fine ashes and sifted them over the ground and the blanketed Apaches. Lee caught the faint odor of the water on the wind. His throat constricted. Lee circled the boulder on silent feet. He stopped short within inches of an Apache who lay face downward with his arms outflung. He died from a knife thrust without opening his eyes.

Metal clicked against stone. An Apache sat up suddenly to look toward the source of the sound. He flung aside his blanket as he stood up, looking about uncertainly. The edge of his blanket rested in the thick ashes. The material began to smolder and then the blanket burst into flames to illuminate the semicircle of boulders. The Apache turned to face Chad's silent charge. Lee closed in behind the buck. Another Apache popped up from behind a ledge near the tanks. He raised a rifle. Lee whirled and drew, firing from the hip. The Apache went down like a jack-in-the-box. Another buck rounded a boulder and aimed a double-barreled shotgun at Lee. Chad's pistol cracked twice right past Lee's head, half deafening him. The Apache went down. His shotgun exploded as it hit the ground. Lee whirled to look for the Apache Chad had charged. The buck was dead across his burning blanket. The shot echoes died away as the acrid gunsmoke arose, mingling with the smoke from the fiercely burning blanket.

"That all of them?" asked Chad in a tense voice.

Lee turned quickly. Two figures broke from cover and legged it toward the brushy slopes. "They're after the horses!" yelled Lee. A rifle flamed from the slope and the first Apache went down to writhe silently on the ground. The second Apache charged up the slope, knife in hand. "Shoot! Shoot! Gawddammit!" yelled Lee.

"It's a woman!" shouted Gil.

"Get her before she reaches you!" roared Chad.

Gil hesitated. The squaw closed in. Gil jumped to one side but he did not fire. Chad fired up the slope and hit her in the back, driving her face downward on the slope. She did not move. Gil ran to her and bent down toward her. The knife fanged upward and caught him across the face. Blood spurted brightly as the kid staggered backward, dropping his rifle. Chad charged up the slope and fired into the woman's back. This time she did not move.

Gil stood there with a dirty hand clamped to the side of his face with the blood leaking between his fingers. Lee came up the slope and pulled the kid's hand aside. He examined the wound. "You'll live," he said dryly. "She broke through the skin. You'll likely have a nice little scar for life, kid."

Gil's eyes were still wide. "She was a woman," he said huskily.

Chad spat to one side. "Some of them are worse than the bucks," he said.

It was very quiet. The wind died away. The blanket burned steadily, casting bright light on the rim of tall boulders and reflecting from the staring eyes of the Apache dead.

"Don't move," warned Chad Mercer.

Lee ignored the order to slowly turn his head. Chad held his cocked Colt not five feet from Lee's back. "Drop that six-gun, Lee," ordered Chad.

The pistol struck the ground. Chad looked up at Gil. "You too, kid," he said. "¡Pronto!" The rifle struck the slope and slid a little way. Chad grinned. "Right into my hands. You stupid bastards, you!" He looked up the slope. "Leila! Bring down that horse and make it quick!"

Hoofs clattered on the loose rock and Leila came slowly down the darkened slope into the faint rim of firelight leading Lee's dun. Her green eyes flicked at Gil and Lee as she halted beside the ring of boulders. She did not look at the sprawled bodies of the dead. The dun shied and blew hard, sidestepping to get away from a body and the smell of its blood.

147

"Get down here, Gil!" ordered Chad. "Fill up those canteens, Leila!"

Gil walked slowly down the slope, shooting a sideways glance at Lee.

"Which way, Chad?" Lee asked pleasantly. "You can't go south or east—the Federales would net you. You can't go west—that's strictly Apache country. North is New Mexico and you know what is waiting for you up there."

Chad looked at Gil. "Go get those Apache horses, kid!"

"Sure, Chad," said Gil. He walked right in front of Chad and between him and Lee. As he did so he back-handed Chad across the nose and eyes. Chad staggered sideways. The kid whirled and sank a pistonlike left into Chad's lean gut just above the belt buckle and as Chad involuntarily bent forward the kid drove up a left upper-cut that connected solidly under Chad's chin, snapping back his head. Chad went flat on the ground, drop-ping his Colt. The kid kicked the Colt toward Lee. Chad rolled sideways onto his feet and caught the kid flatfooted with a left hook that shook him, following through with a right cross that put Gil down on one knee. Gil fell side-ways to avoid a boot aimed at his jaw.

"Help him, Lee!" cried Leila.

Lee shifted his chew and spat. "Help *whom?*" he asked.

Chad moved in, rushing Gil before he could set himself on his feet, striking out with copperhead punches that started to finish the work the squaw's knife had done on Gil's face. Gil staggered back and went down hard. "Get up, you smart young bastard!" snapped Chad. "I ain't done yet!"

The kid did come up, weathered half a dozen punches that *hurt*, clinched with Chad, and overbore him down the slope, then brought up a knee into Chad's privates. Chad grunted in pain and bent forward. A hard young head came up under Chad's chin. He went back and fell to one knee, reaching out for the Colt, but a bootheel caught him right under the left ear and he rolled sideways with wob-bling head and lay still.

Gil stepped back, wiping the blood from his dripping

nose with the back of a hand. His chest rose and fell with his erratic breathing. He ran his tongue along the abraded knuckles of his right hand.

Lee picked up Gil's Colt that had been dropped by Chad. "*Gracias*," he said to Gil.

"*Gracias! Shit!*" said Gil thickly through a mouthful of blood. "Somebody had to stop him and I didn't see you making any heroic moves, big man!" He spat juicily to one side.

"Pretty tough, ain't you?" asked Lee. He grinned.

Gil slowly turned his head. "You want some too?" he asked truculently.

Lee shook his head. "You're too good tonight. You were beginning to take one helluva beating until you got the right idea. Not bad, kid."

"Maybe I have learned something from you," Gil said.

"Took guts to reach across that cocked gun and backhand him like you did."

Gil grinned. "You dumb bastard! That gun was *empty!* You should have figured *that* out. It had only five cartridges in it with the hammer resting on an empty cylinder. I always keep it that way."

Lee pushed out the loading gate and then twirled the cylinder. Each chamber had been loaded. Five of the six cartridges had been fired, but the sixth still had an undented primer. Lee emptied the five brass hulls one by one. They tinkled on the hard ground. Then he tossed the live round to Gil. "You don't count too well, kid. You'd better keep that one for a good luck charm."

Gil caught the cartridge out of the air. His bloody face paled a little. "I suddenly remembered I loaded the sixth chamber up on the rim before I gave the gun to Chad."

"Great time to remember," Lee said. He reloaded his own Colt and walked\over to Chad. He rolled him over and handcuffed him. He did not look at Leila. "Kick that fire into life, kid," ordered Lee over his shoulder. "We'll get something hot to eat, cook some traveling rations, water up, and get to hell out of here before the dawn."

"I'll get the Apache horses first," said Gil. He vanished into the darkness.

Lee walked over to the rock tanks and knelt to fill the canteens. "I suppose you'll never forgive your brother," he said over his shoulder. There was no answer from Leila. Lee filled a cup for her and placed it on a rock. He drank deeply from the tank and then filled the coffeepot with water. He stood up and looked at her. "Well?" he asked at last.

"There's nothing for which to forgive him, Lee," she said quietly.

Chad Mercer sat up. He held his cuffed hands to his smashed mouth. Lee handed Leila a cup of water. "Give him a drink," he suggested. She took the cup and looked at Lee. "I wasn't really sure what kind of a man Chad was until within the past twenty-four hours," she said.

"So?" asked Lee.

"I had your extra pistol in my hands. I could have helped him against you and Gil. I didn't."

"Bitch!" mumbled Chad Mercer.

Lee slowly turned to look at Chad. "Always the gentleman," he commented. "Water him, Leila. We've got to keep him alive until we reach Cibola."

They could hear Gil whistling softly through the darkness as he brought in the Apache horses.

NINETEEN

THERE WAS A SPIT of cold fall rain in the dusk air. A cool wind swept over the rounded hills and swayed the pines and firs thrashing them about and moaning through the darkened meadows. There was a promise of more rain to come.

Lee Kershaw reined in the dun and turned in his saddle to look back over the upturned collar of his coat. "Crossroads," he announced shortly. "Which is it to be? Cibola or the Querencia?"

Gil looked at his sister. "Leila?" he asked.

There was no expression on the face of Chad Mercer. "Cigarette, hombre," he said to Lee.

As Lee shaped the quirly he studied Leila. Far down the tree-clad slopes could be seen the outskirt lights of Cibola winking yellowly through the gathering darkness. Lee leaned toward Chad and placed the cigarette between his lips. Lee thumb-snapped a match into light. Lee cupped the flame in a hand and held it to the tip of the cigarette.

"Leila?" Gil asked again.

Leila looked at Chad. "Will he be all right?" she asked.

Gil nodded. "We'll take him in safely to Dad," he promised.

"Wrong," corrected Lee as he shaped a cigarette for himself. "I'll take him in alone, kid."

Gil turned his head. "I helped," he said.

"It's my job," countered Lee. "You've got a job of your own to do now. A duty, if you like."

"Such as?" queried the kid.

Lee nodded his head toward Leila as he lighted his cigarette. "Take her out to the Querencia. She doesn't really want to go into Cibola to face your father."

"It's not that at all," she said.

"All right, then," said Lee. "Let's get on with it. This wind is cold and the rain is starting to get worse."

Still she hesitated, looking from Lee to Chad and then back to Chad again. Gil leaned over and placed a hand atop hers where they rested folded together on her saddle-horn. "Lee is right," he said. "Come on, sis. It's the best way."

Lee rubbed his face. He was tired. It wasn't really a physical tiredness, although there was plenty of that in his body as well. He had a bone tiredness that was overridden by the tiredness of his mind. He didn't want to think anymore. All he wanted to do now was to get Chad into a warm cell in the Cibola jail and then collect the money due him for bringing Chad back alive. He wanted to have a few drinks, and maybe a lot more, and then to get to hell out of Cibola as though it were cursed with the plague.

Leila raised her head. "I'll come and see you, Chad," she promised, but there didn't seem to be any warmth in her tone.

Chad spat to one side. "Don't bother," he said coldly.

Gil took the reins of Leila's horse and turned it toward the Querencia road. She looked back just once at the two silent men who sat their horses in the drifting rain watching her. In a little while Leila and Gil were out of sight around a turn in the road.

Lee touched the dun with his heels and pulled on the lead reins of Mercer's horse. "A touching scene," said Chad dryly. Lee did not look back at him.

They rode down the last slope and reached the bridge. The river was running fast with ravels of foam slantways across the dark surface of the water. It must be raining hard in the clouded hills.

"Winter's coming on," observed Chad. He looked at Lee. "You'll have it made, back there on the Querencia in that old house with the rain beating on the roof."

"Got to fix the leaks first," Lee said as he rode onto the bridge.

Chad grinned. "The *rancher*," he said.

"Tickles you, does it?" Lee asked.

"I can't help it, hombre."

Lee glanced back at him as they left the bridge. "No hard feelings, eh, hombre?"

"It's your job," replied Chad. He shifted his cigarette from one side of his mouth to the other. "Judas," he added.

A man peered at them through the slowly drifting rain veils and then legged it up the street toward the Granada House. As Lee rode down the center of the rutted street leading Chad's horse with the liquid mud splashing up from the hoofs of the horses he looked neither to the right or the left. By the time he reached the boardwalk in front of the hotel there were four men standing there under the shelter of the porch roof. They were Morgan Beatty, the man named Jed, another hard-faced man Lee did not know and the breed tracker Manuel, who never took his agate eyes off Lee. "Bastard," said Lee under his breath as he dismounted into the ankle-deep mud. Lee looked at Beatty. "Where's Luscombe?" he asked.

"Don't worry," replied Beatty. "He's coming all right. You can turn Mercer over to me."

Lee shook his head. "Not while he's handcuffed and helpless, mister."

"You've got a big mouth, Kershaw."

Lee tilted his head to one side. "You always talk big like that when you're backed by three men?"

Beatty looked quickly away from those cold blue eyes. The misted hotel door swung open. Bennett Luscombe stepped out onto the porch. His dark eyes flicked at Chad Mercer and then at Lee. "Good," he said. "Where are Leila and Gil?"

"Heading for the Querencia—as my guests for the time being, Luscombe," replied Lee.

There was no expression on the sheriff's face. He nodded. "Turn Mercer over to the boys here and then come up to my suite and have a drink. I'd like to hear about what happened."

Lee shook his head. "I'm turning the prisoner Chadwick Mercer over to you, here and now, Sheriff Luscombe, in the presence of these witnesses."

"Very official," said Luscombe. He smiled a little. "I have a proposition for you, Lee. I can use you, if you're interested."

Lee shook his head. He tethered Mercer's horse to the hitching rail

"I owe you money, Kershaw," said Luscombe.

"Deposit it in the bank to my account." Lee looked up at the lawman. "You know now that the Querencia is mine."

"In time," corrected the sheriff.

"It'll be paid for," promised Lee. "I'm even with the board now."

"You won't make the rest of the payments with your income from the ranch," suggested Luscombe.

"I'll pay off," insisted Lee. "One way or another."

Here and there along the street faces were pressed against steamy windows while other men watched from the shelter of doorways.

Lee withdrew the warrant from his inner coat pocket and then unpinned the star from the coat. He handed them both up to the sheriff. "You're making a mistake, Kershaw," warned Luscombe. Lee shook his head. He took out the key to the handcuffs and tossed it to Morgan Beatty. He picked up the reins of the dun and led it away from Chad's horse. "So long, kid," said Lee to Chad. Chad looked down at Lee. There was no expression on his face. "Judas," he said softly. Lee shrugged. He walked through the water-running ruts to the saloon next to the hotel and tethered the dun to the hitching rail under the watchful eyes of the five men on the hotel porch.

Lee pushed through the saloon door. Four men stood just within the front window of the saloon looking throught misted glass at Chad Mercer. "Rye, Buck," said Lee to the bartender. Buck nodded. He placed a full bottle on the mahogany and put a glass beside it. The eyes of the men at the window and those who sat along the long bar slanted toward Lee Kershaw, the tall bearded man who stood there in rain-darkened clothing and mud-caked boots with his eyes seemingly looking into another world beyond the saloon wall. The rain slashed down hard on the roof. No one spoke. The mouth of the rye bottle clinked against the lip of the shot glass at short regular intervals.

A man shouted in the street. Hoofs thudded in the thick mud. A gun exploded. Two more shots cracked out. A man yelled hoarsely. Something fell heavily into the mud just outside of the saloon. Hoofbeats thudded down the street, rattled on the wooden bridge planking, and then died away. It became very quiet in the street.

Lee lowered his glass to the bar. He mechanically wiped his mouth with the back of a hand and then placed a silver dollar beside the bottle. He walked to the door and opened it, then stepped out on the boardwalk. A man lay facedown in the mud fifty feet from the saloon. Four men stood in the street with guns in their hands. Bennett

Luscombe was not in sight. Lee walked to the body and turned it over. The rain beat down suddenly, watering the running blood on the pale face of Chad Mercer.

Boots squelched through the thick mud behind Lee. "He made a break for it, Kershaw," said Morgan Beatty.

Lee looked up into the face of the deputy. "With handcuffed hands?" he quietly asked.

Lee made no move toward the man, but Beatty suddenly stepped back in momentary panic. Lee stood up and walked to his dun. He untethered the dun and mounted it. He touched it with his heels and rode down the center of the street toward the bridge and he did not look back at the curious, staring faces of the swiftly gathering crowd.

TWENTY

THE RAIN WAS slanting down hard and as the cold wind blew the rain it seemed to billow across the dark Querencia Valley. Lee Kershaw crossed the creek bridge and rode up the sloping road to the gateway of his ranch. The windows of the old estancia glimmered with soft yellow lamplight through the sheeting rain. Lee led the dun to the barn and stripped saddle and saddle blanket from him. There were four other horses in the barn stalls. Two of them were those that had been ridden there by Gil and Leila and the third horse was Anselmo Campos' old gray. It was the fourth horse that held Lee's eyes as he rubbed down the dun. The horse was Chad Mercer's fine sorrel; the one he had ridden hard the night he had come to the Querencia for help from his friend Lee Kershaw.

Lee squelched through the mud to the rear door of the casa and hammered on the kitchen door. Gil opened the door. "Where's Leila?" asked Lee in a low voice.

"Lying down."

"And Anselmo?"

Gil grinned a little. "Sitting at the table full of Jerez brandy, dreaming of the old days when he was a *bien parecido*."

Lee walked into the kitchen. He hung his hat on a hook and then peeled off his soaked coat. "You eat?" he asked.

"Blanket steak and corned tomatoes," Gil replied. "There's plenty left. Anselmo drank his supper and Leila didn't eat much."

Lee nodded. "Has the old one drunk up all my booze?"

"There are two bottles in the cabinet."

"Get one," said Lee as he sat down at the table. Anselmo opened his one eye. "*Gracias*," he murmured.

"*Por nada*," replied Gil. He grinned, then looked across the table at Lee. "Well?" he asked.

Lee looked the kid in the eye. "He's dead," he replied. "You?"

Lee shook his head. He downed his drink. "*Ley del fuego*," he said.

"I almost expected that," said Gil. He emptied his glass and then refilled both glasses. "You want to tell her yourself?"

Lee did not answer. He looked down into his glass. "He called me 'Judas,' " he said quietly. "It was the last thing he said to me."

"You were only doing your job, Lee."

"I didn't think they'd kill him like that."

The kid shrugged. "Like you always say to me: 'You ain't too bright.' "

Lee looked at the kid. "Was he guilty?" he asked.

"*¿Quién sabe?*" Gil emptied his glass and reached for the bottle.

"Take it easy, kid," suggested Lee.

"You do your drinking and I'll do mine," retorted Gil.

"Spoken like a man," murmured Lee. He emptied his glass and shook his head as Gil started to fill it. "Wait," he said. "You and your sister had better stay here, for a time at least."

"With you?"

Lee shook his head. "I'm leaving," he said.

"When?"

"Tonight," answered Lee.

Gil studied him. "What about the Querencia?"

"It's mine," replied Lee.

"Maybe Dad doesn't think so."

The look from Lee's blue eyes seemed to strike at the kid. "It's *mine*," repeated Lee.

Gil nodded. "All right, Lee. If you say so." Gil looked toward the darkened hallway. "Maybe she won't want to stay here alone except for Anselmo," he suggested.

"She'll have you, kid."

Gil shook his head. "Crap! I'm going with you."

"No go! I play a lone hand in the manhunting game, kid."

"I'd like some of that good money," said Gil.

"Judas money?" asked Lee. He reached for the bottle and filled his glass.

"It'll pay off the Querencia. Isn't that the whole idea?"

Lee stood up and walked to the stove. He took the lid off the Dutch oven and looked down at the succulent blanket steak. He filled a plate and took it back to the table.

"Well?" asked the kid. "*Isn't* it?"

"Sort of," admitted Lee.

Gil shaped a cigarette. "Maybe she ought to go into Cibola," he suggested. "Dad always liked her better than me." He grinned. "I'm more like Mom, I guess."

"You'd better thank your God for that," mumbled Lee around a mouthful of steak.

"She left him years ago," said Gil.

"You stay here with Leila. She'll need you, kid."

Gil raised a match to his cigarette.

Gil studied his sister. The match seared his fingers. He softly cursed as he threw the match down on the floor. Lee shoved the butter toward him. "You'll need some for that finger," he suggested.

"What happened to Chad?" asked Leila.

Gil glanced at Lee and then at her. "You might as well

know," he replied. "He's dead. *Ley del fuego.* It wasn't Lee."

"I know that," she said. "It was Dad, wasn't it?"

"Morgan Beatty and his 'boys,' " corrected Lee. He did not look at her.

"I expected that," she said quietly.

"You and Gil can stay here as long as you like," he suggested.

"You're leaving, then?" she asked.

Lee nodded. He shoved back his plate, emptied his glass, and then stood up. "You can have the baby here," he said.

"*Gracias*, Lee," she replied.

"*Por nada*, Leila," he said. "I'll need dry clothing. Kid, you stow some grub in a sack for me, along with that extra bottle of Jerez."

"You drink too much," quietly accused Leila.

He shook his head. "Maybe I don't drink enough." He walked past her into the dark hallway. He glanced sideways at her as he did so and the look from her great green eyes made something tighten and slowly turn over deep in his gut.

Leila walked to the table and looked down at her brother. "Well, Gil?" she asked.

Gil nodded. "We'll stay, sis. I ain't about to go back into Cibola and tell Dad you're going to have Chad Mercer's kid out here on the Querencia. Not after Dad just had him '*executed*.' "

"Chad was my husband," she said.

Gil got up without speaking. He filled a sack with canned food, flour, coffee, and other necessaries and placed it on the table with the extra bottle of Jerez.

Spurs softly chimed in the hallway as Lee came back toward the kitchen. He had changed into dry clothing and carried a canvas-wrapped bundle of extra clothing under his arm. He took a slicker from a hook and shrugged into it and then he stowed the brandy bottle into one of the pockets. He picked up the food sack and slung it over a shoulder. "Good luck, Leila," he said. "You'll be all right."

"You should stay and see," she suggested.

Lee shook his head. He looked down at Anselmo Campos. "Good-bye, old one," he said quietly.

Anselmo raised his head, downed his drink, and placed the empty glass on the table. "*Vaya con Dios, patrón,*" he said.

Lee gripped the old man's shoulder for a second or two. "See that he gets his brandy, kid," he said. "He asks for nothing else." Lee walked to the door. "I'll send back money for the ranch payments," he said. "On time." He smiled. Neither Leila nor Gil spoke as Lee walked out onto the porch.

Lee walked through the rain to the barn. He saddled the sorrel that had belonged to Chad and then stowed away his food and clothing. He hung his scabbarded Winchester to the saddle.

The barn door creaked back. "She wants you to stay, Lee," said the kid.

Lee took out his tobacco canteen and a packet of cigarette papers and began to shape a cigarette. "No," he replied. "Not now anyway. Later, perhaps, kid, but not now."

Gil studied Lee. "You're sure that was not a real priest who married them?" he asked.

Lee nodded. "Positive!"

"Should I tell her?"

Lee lighted the cigarette and studied Gil over the flare of the match. "That's up to you, kid."

"Dammit! I'm asking *you!*"

Lee shrugged. "What's the difference now? Both Padre Antonio and Chad Mercer are dead. You and me are the only living persons who know the truth. Let the kid have a name, Gil."

"He'll need a father someday, Lee," suggested Gil. He ran a hand down the neck of the sorrel. "Maybe a man like you," he added.

"Leila might have something to say about that."

"You ain't too bright, amigo."

Lee took the reins and led the sorrel to the open doorway. The rain slanted down hard. "I'll write out a will," Lee said over his shoulder. "You and your sister will get the Querencia if anything happens to me, kid."

"That isn't necessary, Lee."

"I haven't got anyone else, kid," said Lee. "Just take care of Anselmo for me." He led the horse out into the rain and mounted it. He looked down at the kid.

"You *are* coming back, aren't you Lee?" asked Gil.

Lee nodded. "It's my Querencia, isn't it?"

"If you say so, Lee."

"So long, kid."

"*Vaya con Dios*, amigo!"

Gil stood in the doorway of the barn and watched Lee as he rode slowly through the slanting gray veils of rain. Lee paused at the gate, withdrew the brandy bottle from his slicker pocket, and drank deeply. He replaced the bottle in the pocket, wiped his mouth, and then rode on, vanishing into the rain and the darkness of the night.

Gil put out the lantern and closed the barn door. He squelched through the mud toward the house. He stopped in the shelter of the ramada roof at the front of the house and looked down the dark slopes toward the creek bridge. He could hear the rushing of the rapidly rising creek and the moaning of the cold night wind, but there was no sight or sound of Lee Kershaw. There were voices in the night wind, but Gil could not interpret them as he could not interpret the man Lee Kershaw. He closed the door behind him, shutting off the yellow rectangle of lamplight. Darkness closed in thickly over the rain-soaked Valley of the Querencia.